AN UNBREAKABLE BOND

TURNBULL

D1386623

There was nothing wrong with Tiffany's friendship with Geoffrey Upcott—they were just two lonely people who liked each other. So why did his nephew, Eliot, disapprove? And did he have to show his contempt for her quite so blatantly?

Books you will enjoy
by ROBYN DONALD

THE GATES OF RANGITATAU

Brokenhearted over the way Greg Bardsley had deceived her, Christabel had behaved very foolishly with Alex Thomassin—and as a result of it all she had left Australia and taken refuge with her family back in New Zealand. There she began to find peace again—until that peace was destroyed in the most unexpected manner . . .

A DURABLE FIRE

Arminel liked Rhys Beringer, enough to accept his invitation to visit his family home in New Zealand—but not enough to marry him. But his cold brother Kyle chose to misinterpret the situation and to think the very worst of her. Yet it was Kyle with whom she fell in love—to her lasting regret . . .

AN
UNBREAKABLE
BOND

BY

ROBYN DONALD

MILLS & BOON LIMITED
15–16 BROOK'S MEWS
LONDON W1A 1DR

All the characters in this book have no existence outside
the imagination of the Author, and have no relation
whatsoever to anyone bearing the same name or names.
They are not even distantly inspired by any individual
known or unknown to the Author, and all the incidents
are pure invention.

The text of this publication or any part thereof may not
be reproduced or transmitted in any form or by any
means, electronic or mechanical, including photocopying,
recording, storage in an information retrieval system, or
otherwise, without the written permission of the publisher.

This book is sold subject to the condition that it shall not,
by way of trade or otherwise, be lent, resold, hired out or
otherwise circulated without the prior consent of the
publisher in any form of binding or cover other than that
in which it is published and without a similar condition
including this condition being imposed on the subsequent
purchaser.

First published in Great Britain 1986
by Mills & Boon Limited

© Robyn Donald 1986

Australian copyright 1986
Philippine copyright 1986
This edition 1986

ISBN 0 263 75301 8

Set in Monophoto Times 10 on 10 pt.
01-0386 – 61481

Made and printed in Great Britain by
Richard Clay (The Chaucer Press) Ltd,
Bungay, Suffolk

CHAPTER ONE

To someone accustomed to life in a small mining and farming community on the west coast of the South Island, Auckland, New Zealand's biggest city, was a revelation: not, in spite of its superb position on two harbours and its almost sub-tropical climate, a particularly pleasant one.

After a month Tiffany Brandon was at last able to sleep through the night without being disturbed by the unfamiliar noises of the traffic, but although she was learning to appreciate this sprawling bustling city, she still missed her home and its quiet peacefulness.

Especially she longed for her mother and her two younger half-brothers, John and Peter. At thirteen and eleven, their noise and high spirits had often irritated her; now she wished fervently that she could hear them as they tormented her one more time. And although she had never understood the big, reserved man who was her stepfather, she found herself missing him too. Rigid, even inflexible, George might be, but he was familiar and that meant that he was dear to her.

Never before in her life had she been lonely. Now it was like an ache in her heart. She didn't have much in common with the other girls in the hostel. They, too, came from country districts, but most of them from quite close to Auckland. In Tiffany's great dark eyes they seemed extremely sophisticated, talking only of boyfriends and love affairs and the latest trends. They were pleasant, but so busy!

At work it was much the same. She was the youngest, and the only single one, and her fellow seamstresses had interests which were concentrated on their families.

What she was suffering from, of course, was a massive dose of homesickness. It would fade and in time die; in the meantime she looked forward to her lunchtimes, for then she took her sandwiches to a small park down the road and quite often found there the only friend she had made yet in Auckland.

The girls in the hostel would have been rather disdainful of Mr Upcott. He was definitely masculine, but, at a good forty years older than Tiffany's twenty-two, not the age to interest them. Tiffany, however, had realised that he, too, was lonely and had proffered her quick, shy smile. Their acquaintance had progressed from smiles to words, from thence to long conversations. Gradually they had progressed further to something like friendship. Each day Tiffany found herself looking forward to her lunchtime, for he was an interesting conversationalist, treating her with an old-world courtesy which she liked.

Today he was waiting for her, dapper in a suit which was certainly not new but which bore the undefinable stamp of a good tailor.

'How pretty you look,' he said, getting to his feet as she came towards him. 'Like spring on this lovely autumn day.'

She smiled, the depths of her eyes aglimmer with tiny gold sparks. 'Thank you. You look very smart, too.'

'Oh, I have to go into town later.' He waited until she had sat down before re-seating himself. 'Tell me, are you settling in? You seem to be losing that rather *triste* look I noticed when we first met.'

'Oh, I'm getting used to the life.' She opened her lunchbox with neat, precise movements, eyeing its contents with distaste. The hostel provided a packed lunch every day, but it was made with startling lack of imagination.

'Happier? Not quite so homesick?'

She gave him her bright smile. 'Yes, although the girls in the hostel still consider me the original hick. They're very nice to me, just the same.'

'What made you decide to come up to Auckland?'

Her slender shoulders lifted then fell. 'There was nothing for me at home. When I left school my stepfather found me a job in an accountant's office; I was lucky to get that.'

'I was an accountant, you know.' Before she could do more than show her surprise he sent her a quick, understanding smile. 'Well, a kind of one. Didn't you like it?'

'No. I wanted to do things with my hands. I've always been able to sew and embroider, dream up different ways of doing things like that. My stepfather thinks it's a frivolous little talent and I suppose it is, but it's the only one I've got and I wanted to use it. I felt that if I didn't get away I'd dwindle into—into a nothing.' She gestured with her small, capable hands, trying rather helplessly to explain. 'Don't get me wrong, it's a lovely place to live, but I wanted to see if I could—I felt that I had to get away. It was stifling me.'

The sudden passion in her voice startled her as much as it did him. 'Sorry,' she said shamefacedly. 'My stepfather is always on at me for dramatising. But I really did feel that I needed to leave home.'

'Oh, don't apologise.' His intelligent eyes rested thoughtfully on her irregular profile. 'I'm just a little surprised to find an ardent temperament beneath that serene face, that's all.'

'Well, I try to keep it under control,' she told him ruefully.

'And succeed admirably. Why Auckland, though? It's such a long way from home.'

The sun struck sparks from her black curls as she nodded. 'My mother suggested it, surprisingly enough; much to my stepfather's horror. He's a dear, but terribly old-fashioned and—and *good*. He thinks cities are hot beds of sin, and Auckland especially so, but Mum said that if I wanted to get anywhere Auckland was the logical place to come. She came up with me and organised this job as seamstress at Jackson's and found the hostel for me to board in.'

'And how do you like sewing curtains and cushions and upholstery for an interior decorating shop?'

She shrugged again, her expression revealing her emotions. 'Well, it's a living, and I am learning a lot.'

'What would you really like to do, Tiffany?'

'Make pretty things,' she replied promptly. 'Since I've been at Jackson's I've seen such a lot of lovely things: table mats and napkins, tablecloths and bed covers, cushions, that sort of thing. I'd like to supply decorators like Jackson's and a few shops with things like that. One-off, special things. I could do it.' Her soft mouth firmed. 'I'm going to do it, one day.'

'Bravo,' he encouraged softly. 'Would it pay?'

'Oh yes.' She turned to him, her face alight with eagerness. 'Some women don't care what they pay for things that catch their eye. They don't even care about the workmanship, providing it looks good and is different.'

Her pretty voice stumbled slightly as she told him of several customers who seemed to use the shop as a way of filling in time, magpies buying whatever took their fancy without regard for price or quality.

The sun danced on the thick curls over her small, poised head and gilded the pale olive of her skin. She had an unusual face, oddly young for a girl who had passed her twenty-second birthday. No one could have called her beautiful; she knew that she was not even pretty and if anyone had told her that she pleased the eye she would have laughed at them. But it was true that her voice was unusual, deep and delightful to listen to, and she was the lucky possessor of a freshness which appealed to those who looked any deeper than the surface. Now, animated and unselfconscious, she made a striking picture.

When she had finished, Geoffrey Upcott smiled with a rather bitter irony. 'I know the sort. Women like that must make Peter Jackson very happy,' he observed. His head moved; the old eyes looked beyond her as he continued, 'Ah, here comes my lift into town. Early, I'm afraid.'

His lift turned out to be a man, a very tall man who

moved with lithe graceful strides across the grass. Her eyes dazzled by the sun, Tiffany looked up into a face which seemed carved out of stone, the harshly-outlined, autocratic features subordinated to eyes of a brilliant, blazing blue and a mouth which was thin and straight and hard. He was not handsome but that fact did not register. Such authority emanated from him that Tiffany felt almost totally intimidated.

Unconsciously her chin came up. She met the speculation in his stare with a composure which took all of her strength to maintain.

'Ah, Eliot,' Mr Upcott greeted him cheerfully. 'Early as ever. Tiffany, this is my nephew, Eliot Buchanan. Eliot, you've heard of Tiffany Brandon who kindly allows some of her lunch hours to be monopolised by me.'

For some reason Tiffany did not want to shake hands with Eliot Buchanan. Of course she had to, even though the touch of his tanned strong fingers about hers sent a hot little shudder across her skin.

'Miss Brandon,' he said with remote courtesy, the smile on his lips strangely narrow. 'Do you work around here?'

He spoke with a cutting edge to his beautiful voice which furthered her first impression of him as a dangerous man. Tiffany's skin tightened and she pulled her hand away. He was being patronising and he knew it, and he intended her to know it too.

'Yes,' she said. 'Do you, Mr Buchanan?'

Those vivid eyes flamed before dark, thick lashes came down over them. 'Why, no,' he said softly. 'My office is in town.'

Naturally. He wore a dark, elegantly cut suit which had probably cost more than her stepfather spent on clothes in ten years. Probably, she decided waspishly and quite unfairly, it was his tailor's skill which made her feel that there was a body of whiplash power beneath the beautiful fabric.

Almost she flinched as his eyes ran over her in a

comprehensive assessment before dismissing her. As dusky colour scorched up through her skin he turned to his uncle, saying, 'Time we went, I'm afraid. You won't want to miss your appointment.'

'Oh, doctors always keep you waiting,' the older man returned cheerfully, 'Still, I suppose we'd better go. Goodbye, Tiffany.'

'Goodbye, Mr Upcott.' She paused before adding, 'Goodbye, Mr Buchanan.'

He appeared astonished that she should address him, lifting dark brows as he replied, 'Goodbye, Tiffany,' thereby underlining the social gap between them with a total lack of subtlety. His uncle looked sharply at him but beyond proffering an apologetic smile to Tiffany he made no remonstrance as his nephew led him off.

Not that he did, of course. Eliot Buchanan did not touch his uncle, but there was no doubt that he was shepherding him away as quickly as he could, as if her presence was a contamination.

Tiffany felt a hot wave of humiliation, but beneath it was anger and a cold pride. Who did Mr Eliot Buchanan think he was? He had deliberately tried to make her feel inferior; succeeded, too, although her brain told her that such an attitude was out-of-date. That was what money and social position did to you, she thought: bred arrogance and a snobbish intolerance. It wasn't even as though he was much older than her—no more than ten years. Yet he had made it quite clear that as far as he was concerned the gulf between them was unbridgeable.

She stayed on the bench, her eyes fixed on the two figures as they walked across to where a very opulent car waited. From her perusal of one of her brother John's books she thought that it might be a Lotus. Whatever, it looked big and powerful and horrendously expensive.

As she watched, Eliot Buchanan stooped to unlock the passenger's side then swung around the long bonnet to do the same to his door. The benign autumn sun picked out mahogany highlights in his dark hair. As if her gaze was tangible, he looked over. She saw the white flash of teeth as he smiled, and then he was in the car and it was pulling away from the kerb.

The gentle curve of Tiffany's mouth tightened, then relaxed. Stupid to allow the man to upset her. The world was structured, always had been. Even at Jackson's there were quite rigid demarcation lines. The decorators considered themselves a step above the shop assistants; the assistants were certain that they had more status than the women who worked in the sewing room. And there the married women felt a little superior to her, the only single one. No one ever remarked on it; the system was just accepted. Looked at the right way it was a spur to ambition.

As of now. To her surprise Tiffany found herself vowing that one day Eliot Buchanan would look at her and find no cause for such supercilious scorn.

Somewhat taken aback by the fierceness with which she made her promise to destiny, she crumpled a crust in her hand, dropping the crumbs for the cheeky sparrows before she got to her feet.

It was pay-day, and she had money to put in the bank. Her heart was set on buying an industrial sewing machine and the one she wanted was expensive enough to need quite a few months of hard saving.

Mr Upcott made no appearance the next day, or the next. In fact it was a week before he came to the park and somehow in that week he seemed to have shrunk, become tired and older.

When she saw him waiting for her on the park bench Tiffany was surprised at the sudden lift of her spirits. She had become fond of him, and had missed him.

She made no attempt to hide her pleasure, smiling at him with such warmth that his answering smile was slightly startled.

'How charming you look,' he said; his usual remark but delivered with such gallantry that he made it fresh and sincere each time.

Tiffany laughed. Her clothes were pretty and modest but far from fashionable. 'Why, thank you. Are you sure it isn't just the day? I know it's autumn, but I find it awfully hard to believe that winter will soon be here. It's still so warm and the days are so beautifully clear.'

'Ah, that's autumn. During summer the sky is usually hazy, and it's a lot hotter and more humid.' He nodded at her bag. 'Have you had lunch?'

'No, I'm going to eat it now. I'm starving.'

While she unwrapped her sandwiches he spoke easily, lightly, of happenings in and around the city. It was quite obvious that he kept his fingers on the pulse of events; obvious, too, that he knew many of the people he spoke of. Tiffany had never thought of his background, just accepting him as a fellow sufferer of loneliness, but Eliot Buchanan's obvious wealth had made her wonder why Mr Upcott was reduced to chatting to a girl he'd met on a park bench for company.

'You're looking rather pensive,' he observed.

She wiped her fingers on a tissue, wondering if he would think her presumptuous. After a moment she said, 'I was wondering how your appointment at the doctor's went.'

'Oh, that.' He smiled wryly. 'Just a check up. As I expected, I had to wait. Eliot is a very impatient man. He is my late wife's nephew—she and his mother were sisters. That makes him feel he can order me around.'

'He seemed a bit overbearing,' she agreed, cautiously, because it was obvious that he admired and respected his nephew.

'Yes.' He chuckled. 'His manner can be off-putting. That's what being a lawyer does to you: makes you profoundly suspicious of motives and actions.'

'I noticed.'

If he heard the thread of anger in her voice he chose to ignore it. 'He's brilliant, Eliot. Sharp, and very, very hard to fool. He would have made a spectacular criminal lawyer, but he felt duty-bound to manage the family holdings. They're an extremely wealthy lot, the

Buchanans, and Eliot looks after everything, stocks, shares, several big farms and orchards, oh, an assortment of businesses. He's a tough man, but supremely trustworthy, with the sort of integrity which makes him rather uncomfortable company for we less incorruptible mortals.' He sat silently musing before resuming, 'But there's no need for you to worry about Eliot and his arrogant ways. I came to ask you if you'd have dinner with me tomorrow night.'

Astonishment rounded her mouth and eyes.

Chuckling, he said drily, 'No, I'm not a dirty old man, I promise you. It's just that I have a burden I've been carrying around for years and I think you might be able to help me with it.'

Naturally she was curious. Certainly she was, in the light of later events, somewhat naïve, but she followed her instinct to trust him and that at least didn't let her down. It didn't occur to her that others might put the wrong construction on their dinner together, not even when the taxi he sent delivered her to one of a row of expensive town houses in a very exclusive suburb. After all, Eliot Buchanan had been an intimation of the social circle his uncle moved in. But even if she hadn't met the nephew she would have recognised the easy assurance which made Mr Upcott different from any other man she had known.

Dinner was superbly cooked, and Tiffany enjoyed it. She enjoyed herself, too. Her host offered her wine, but didn't seem surprised when she refused it. Although her stepfather was a teetotaller she knew that her mother didn't hold such rigid views on alcohol, but she didn't want to reveal her complete ignorance. Mr Upcott didn't drink either, until after dinner when he settled her down before the fire with coffee. With his he had brandy, a tiny amount which he obviously enjoyed.

Tiffany gazed around the lovely, carefully furnished room. Outside a small wind had risen, but here it was warm and comfortable. She smiled at her host, her affection and contentment clear.

'Tell me about your name,' he said, setting down his coffee cup with a small, sharp movement. 'It's very pretty. Tiffany is a contraction of Theophania, I believe.'

She laughed. 'Oh, no. Well, it may be, but my proper name is Tifaine. My mother told me that it was my father's grandmother's name and he wanted me to be called after her because he was very fond of her.' She stared into the leaping flames, her expression wistful. 'I think Mum must have loved him very much because it hurt her to talk about him. After a while I didn't ask. But I do know that he had an unhappy childhood and that his grandmother loved him and was kind to him. He died before I was born.'

'Did he?' There was an odd note in his voice which caught her attention, but he wasn't looking at her. His fingers stroked the smooth, foxy head of his small corgi bitch as he said. 'My grandmother's name was Tifaine. She had eyes like yours, so dark that you couldn't tell if they were black or brown, and like you, hers had tiny glints of gold in the darkness. When she was angry they used to flare up like small flames.'

Tiffany's breath caught in her throat. She made a funny little noise in her throat and he lifted his head to look at her with something like pleading in his eyes.

'What—it can't—I can't——' she whispered, her brain unable to accept what he was trying to tell her.

'Your mother wrote to me when she was in Auckland,' the even, masculine voice said remorselessly. 'She couldn't bring herself to confess to you, although I'm quite sure that she had no need to worry. I'm certain you won't despise her for what she did.'

'Mum and—and you?' It was too much. She burst into tears, her black curls trembling as she bowed her head into the sofa cushions.

He let her weep for some time to the accompaniment of the crackling of the fire and the dog's uneasy whining, but when her storm of tears showed no signs of abating he came over to sit beside her, saying quietly,

'Hush, now, my dear. You'll give yourself a headache if you keep it up for much longer.'

She accepted the handkerchief he gave her and began to mop up, trying rather desperately to control her sobs. He made her sip some brandy, insisting when she objected, then held her hand until the convulsive movements stopped.

Then he asked, 'May I tell you how it happened? If, after that, you want to go home I'll ring for a taxi and you needn't worry about ever seeing me again. I hope you'll find it in your heart to forgive us both.'

It was a common enough story. A man locked in an unhappy marriage by convention and his children; his secretary newly come from another city and lonely. They had been drawn into each other's arms by a strong physical attraction and a need for comfort.

'When she told me that she was pregnant I offered to divorce my wife,' he told Tiffany, his expression bleak as he reviewed that comfortless time. 'Marie refused. She did not love me and she was wise enough to know that marriage between us would not work. Besides, my wife would have—well, she did not want a divorce. Marie went to Wellington, to a friend she had there. I supported her, of course. When you were born she wrote to me that you were beautiful, black-eyed and black-haired, with olive skin. I asked her to call you Tifaine.'

Tiffany nodded, gulping a little, the eyes she shared with her great-grandmother fixed on his face.

'As Marie told you, my childhood was—grim. About the only bright spot in it was my grandmother. I had wanted to name a daughter after her but my wife found the name too outrageous. She called our children Diane and Colin. I'm glad now. Diane looks like her mother, but you are my grandmother all over again.' His look was affectionate and reminiscent. 'She was descended from a French family which is where the name comes from. She was a little body, like you, with the same warm smile and pretty voice.'

'I'm—I'm glad.'

He surveyed her with a mixture of yearning and regret. 'Are you, Tiffany? I hope so. I do realise what a shock this has been to you.'

'Why didn't Mum tell me that you were still alive? I used to wonder what my father was like. I can see why she didn't want to talk about you—and I suppose I know why she pretended to be a widow. But I wish I'd known. All she ever told me about my father was that he was kind and clever.'

His smile was ironic, but tinged with sadness. 'She is kind, too,' he said, and there was a silence, heavy with memories, until Tiffany asked,

'Has she kept in touch with you?'

'No. As soon as you reached school age she went to the South Island and refused any further support. She wrote that she thought it best for everyone if she cut the connection completely. At the time my life was in an upheaval. I'm afraid I was rather relieved. For quite a few years I almost managed to forget your existence. Not quite, however.'

Tiffany looked down at his hand. An old man's hand with enlarged knuckles and age spots, but when she held hers against it they were the same, the fingers tapering, the little finger exactly the same length as the forefinger on the left, and slightly shorter on the right.

Perhaps it was that which convinced her. She swallowed and looked up at him, her eyes misty.

'I wish I'd known,' she said. 'It would have been—nice.'

He nodded. 'I'm sorry,' he said simply.

She shook her head. 'No, don't be. I had a happy childhood. I just used to wonder about my father.'

'Well, now you know.'

Silence fell, a strangely comfortable silence. The logs on the fire crackled softly before subsiding into a soft, purring hiss. Spread out on the carpet the dog, a friendly, pretty corgi called Jess, lay on her back, short legs held in the air in a manner which looked profoundly uncomfortable but clearly wasn't. It was strange how easily Tiffany accepted the fact that this man was her father; she felt at home here.

After a while she said, 'You said Mother wrote to you. When was this?'

'When she came up to settle you in. She said that she would feel happier about leaving you here if she knew there was someone to look out for you. She gave me the choice of meeting you or not.' He sighed. 'I was surprised to discover that I had a very strong desire to know my other daughter.'

'So you sought me out.'

'Yes. I thought it would be easier for you if I gave you a chance to like me first.'

Tiffany nodded. Probably he had wanted to find out what this unknown daughter of his was like before he committed himself in any way. A little hard-headed but a sensible reaction just the same.

'Tiffany, is your mother happy?'

She looked surprised, her dark eyes suddenly wary. 'Yes. Yes, she seems to be. Why?'

'Because in her letter she asked that we don't make our relationship public. And the reason she gave is that her husband would find it hard to forgive her for the deception she practised.'

'The deception—oh, of course. I suppose he accepted that she was a widow just as I did.' Tiffany frowned, her stepfather's face coming to mind. 'Yes,' she said slowly, reluctantly. 'He's very—very rigid in his views. He would find a lie like that abhorrent.'

'And the fact that you—that there was no marriage?'

Tiffany frowned. 'I think he would probably be unable to accept that, too,' she said. 'He is—he's very *good* himself, very straight, and although he would probably forgive my mother he might not ever be able to fully trust her again.'

'Poor Marie,' her father said quietly. 'Then we must not destroy her happiness. Unfortunately, that means that the exact relationship between us will have to remain ambiguous. And that will give rise to talk.'

The swift colour flushed across Tiffany's skin but she said stoutly, 'I don't care, if you don't.'

'I'm afraid you don't have much idea of what it's likely to be like,' he told her wearily. 'Gossip of the nastiest sort. And as I cannot risk telling my son and daughter about you, there will be unpleasantness there, too.'

Something in his voice brought her head swinging around. 'You sound as though you don't like them much,' she said uncertainly. 'Or trust them.'

'Astute of you. No, I do not. I'm afraid that they— well, I believe that between us their mother and I ruined them. They grew up in an atmosphere of suspicion and dislike. Both of us tried to compensate by indulging them, with the usual results.'

'Well, I don't have to meet them,' Tiffany said robustly, her tones coloured by the sudden realisation of just what was likely to lie in front of her.

'I think it best if you don't.' He sighed and took her hands in his, holding her eyes with his shrewd, worldly gaze. 'Perhaps you had better think it over, Tiffany. No, don't say yes yet. You're off balance at the moment. The taxi will be here any minute to take you back to the hostel. When you are there think very carefully. If you see any more of me then our visits in the park there will be innuendoes—malice and sneers. I don't want you hurt. I'll understand if you don't want to lay yourself open to that sort of thing. You owe me nothing.'

But he looked lonely as he waved goodbye: lonely and old and tired. Perhaps Tiffany's mind was made up for her then by her last glimpse of him, with only the little dog for company, a thin dark figure against the light.

Perhaps it was what happened when she made her way to the park the next day. It was cooler, a day of bright sunshine with great galleons of cloud propelled across the blue, clear sky by a brisk southerly wind. Although the gardens were still bright with asters and dahlias it was easy to accept that winter was not far distant.

As usual he was waiting for her on the bench. Tiffany hurried towards him, her smile irradiating her face, the wind tossing her short black curls and whipping vivid colour into her cheeks.

When she came closer her steps faltered, for it was not her father who sat on the bench but his nephew. He lounged back on the seat, long legs extended, his expression almost predatory. When she came up he remained as he was, those brilliant eyes very insolent as they scanned her face.

Her first reaction was panic. 'Is—is there something wrong?' she asked unevenly. He stared at her, his dark, straight brows raised in haughty enquiry. Flushing, she stammed, 'My—Mr Upcott—is he all right? Not sick or—or anything?'

'Not sick—not even tired.' The words were cool and deliberate, tinged with scorn. 'Do sit down, Tiffany. You remind me of a flamingo, hopping from one leg to the other.'

Her mouth tightened but she obeyed his lazy gesture, sitting as far away from him as the bench allowed. He smiled without humour, his gaze moving slowly over her face and body. It was a piece of calculated rudeness which brought the blood beating up into her skin.

'Charming,' he drawled, obviously not meaning it. 'Yes, I can see what Geoffrey wants. Your youth and that air of naïve freshness. What I fail to understand is what you see in him. The money, I suppose.' He was watching her keenly with half-closed eyes, watching as the colour faded from her skin, leaving her sallow and pinched looking.

'He has a lot of money,' he went on softly, 'but he was not an extremely successful accountant for nothing, you know. If you expect to get rich from him, think again.'

So it had started. The knowing, cynical expression he wore made her feel sick but she lifted her head proudly.

'Aren't you making assumptions out of turn?'

'My dear, I know that you went to his house last night and didn't get back until after eleven,' he said in the most bored voice she had ever heard. He leaned back against the seat, stuffing his hands into his pockets. From beneath lashes too long and thick for a man he watched her, eyes narrowed against the sun's glare.

Tiffany felt absurdly guilty—and angry.

'Did you enjoy your snooping, Mr Buchanan?'

He smiled maliciously. 'I've far better things to do than follow a pretty little tramp around Auckland,' he told her gently, watching with the eye of a connoisseur as she bit her lip and looked away. 'A couple of phone calls was enough.'

Deep in her eyes tiny glints sparkled into life. A cold rage possessed her. With a swift movement she got to her feet.

'Goodbye, Mr Buchanan,' she said clearly and walked swiftly away, back held so rigid that she felt as though it might snap.

She didn't expect him to follow so that his voice from immediately behind her made her stumble. Instantly she was caught, steadied, and then released from hands as strong and hurtful as steel.

'Go away,' she said with icy clarity.

He looked down at her, all expression gone from the harsh symmetry of his features.

'When you've listened to what I have to say. If you're as innocent as those blushes suggest it may save you heartache.'

She hesitated and he said gravely, 'I think you had better, Tiffany. Where are your parents?'

'In the South Island.'

He looked at her for a long moment then gave a coaxing, completely irresistible smile. 'They shouldn't have let you come here by yourself,' he said. 'How old are you?'

Tiffany blinked, stunned by this completely unexpected charm. Her eyes widened as she answered, 'Twenty-two.' Adding with a flash of spirit, 'Which is not too young to be tipped out of the nest.'

'Is that what happened?' he asked. 'Were you tipped out of the nest?'

'*No!* I was—I was speaking figuratively.'

That smile lingered, transforming him into the most attractive man she had ever met. It was rather frightening to see such a metamorphosis.

'I see,' he said blandly, not bothering to hide the amusement in his eyes. 'A very sheltered twenty-two years, I think. It's certainly time that someone taught you the facts of life, but it shouldn't be Geoffrey, you know.'

'But he's not——' She stopped, and looked away, miserably aware that she had to keep her mother's secret.

'Because he's old enough to be your father?' His voice was gentle yet there was a hint of condescension in the deep tones which set her hackles rising. Before she had time to say anything he continued, 'Surely your mother warned you that the big city is full of bad men, all of them panting to get you into bed? And that being a grandfather doesn't depress desire completely? Geoffrey is well aware of the fact that you have a slim supple body, with skin like satin and eyes dark enough to drown in and a mouth that asks to be kissed into silence. We discussed you on the way into Auckland the other day.'

'I don't believe you,' she said huskily, angry and sickened at the contemptuous amusement in his words. 'You're—I won't listen to you saying such horrible things. You're not a particularly loyal nephew, are you?'

'Oh, I'm a man of the world,' he said, openly mocking her. 'So is Geoffrey. You won't be the first, you know. Since my aunt's death there have been quite a few women in Geoffrey's life. All of them considerably younger than he is. He's always been that way. My aunt was quite a bit younger than him.'

'I don't have to listen to this—this nastiness,' she retorted contemptuously, turning away from him. The charm had gone for her now; there was nothing she wanted more than to fling the truth of her relationship with his uncle at him but, as she could not, she could only express her outrage and dislike.

His hand on her elbow made her jump. It wasn't painful but she could feel impatience in the long fingers and in spite of herself she froze. Some instinct warned her that at that moment he badly wanted to hurt her and would use the smallest excuse to do it.

'Yes, you do,' he said silkily, his expression darkening. 'You stupid little idiot, can't you see——'

'All I can see is a man who is interfering in something that doesn't concern him,' she interrupted, the sparks in her glance dancing as she glared up at him. A desire to pay him back for his high-handed intolerance drove her recklessly on. 'Have Geoffrey's family appointed you to watch their interests? They should have chosen a more conciliatory emissary. I may be naïve and come from the sticks, but I dislike being patronised just as much as anyone who was born and bred in Auckland.'

'Did I say that you were naïve?' he returned, all expression gone from his face. His gaze narrowed into a scrutiny so intense that she felt as though he was stripping her. 'How stupid of me,' he said quite softly. 'It must be a very useful stock-in-trade, that ability to blush. All right, Tiffany. How much?'

The sudden change to a crisp, icy formality made her jaw drop. Like the country girl he had thought her she stood gaping at him until the insult registered. Then she swallowed, her hands clenching into fists.

'Come on,' he said impatiently, 'There's no need for any further pretence. You almost had me fooled, you know; you should really try to get into television. Soap operas would offer an excellent vehicle for talents like yours.'

'Why—you—you——'

'How much?' He cut her short, his voice and face

bored as he named a sum which made her gape again. 'Think about it,' he commanded. 'It's quite a reasonable amount and you won't have to go to bed with an old man to get it.'

'You have a mind like a sewer,' she said shakily, appalled at the crude directness of his bargaining.

'I'm a realist. Don't make up your mind yet.' He smiled sardonically as she pushed a damp curl back from her temple. 'I'll take you out to dinner tonight and you can give me your answer then.'

Something in the way he was looking at her made her uneasy. 'No thanks,' she said shortly.

'You could do much better for yourself than Geoffrey,' he told her blandly, the heavy-lidded eyes almost closed as they surveyed her flushed face.

'If you mean what I think, then the answer is definitely no.' Incredibly, her voice was unwavering. It can't be happening to me, she thought raggedly. But it was. She, reserved Tiffany Brandon, whose only experience of love had been some not too serious kissing, had been mistaken for a—a whore, to use the most basic word, and was now being propositioned by the most attractive, detestable man she had ever met.

'I think you would enjoy the alternative more than the route you've chosen,' he said calmly, his gaze making it quite obvious what he was talking about. 'Geoffrey is not senile—or incompetent—but he is old. However fit, a certain lack of—shall we call it vitality— is characteristic after fifty.'

The permissive generation had passed Tiffany by. Oh, she had read about the new freedoms but the small town where she spent her formative years had been untouched by them and because of her stepfather's outlook she was less experienced that most girls of her age. Now Eliot Buchanan had forced her to confront an ugly reality, his cynical sophistication ripping her quiet innocence into shreds. At that moment she hated him, a hatred made even stronger by the tiny pull of attraction she had felt when he had smiled at her. That had been deliberate, of course. He had wanted to charm her into surrender and to do it had consciously summoned charisma he must have used thousands of times before.

'Perhaps,' she said coldly, 'that's what I want.' She wondered why she was baiting him. The safest thing to do would be to go; he could do nothing to her here, even though his face, his whole stance told her that at that moment what he wanted more than anything was to hurt her.

'I see,' he said with savage contempt. 'You aren't even prepared to earn your money fairly. Well, so be it. Battle is joined. Don't come whining to me for mercy at any stage because there will be none. By the time I've finished with you, Tiffany, you'll wish you'd taken my offer.' He laughed between his teeth at her swift backwards step. 'And I might even have you, at that. You can't have learned much about sex yet and Geoffrey certainly won't have the stamina to further your education. If I take you in hand you'll be capable of satisfying the most jaded palate.'

'Let me go.' She jerked her elbow free, frightened by the cold sensuality of his words and face.

For a moment they stared at each other, he tall and overpowering, her slender young body held straight against the waves of fury she could feel emanating from him, her hands clenched against her sides, her eyes refusing to surrender.

'You can go to—to hell,' she flung clearly, then turned and walked away, spoiling the thin defiance of her parting line with the speed of her departure.

She could feel him watching her; the tiny hairs on the back of her neck and down her spine were lifted and tense as she walked swiftly down beneath the yellowing trees to the big single camellia at the gate. From the first few rose-pink flowers with their gold stamens came a fresh, earthy fragrance like a flower shop. Usually Tiffany stopped and admired the crinkled silk petals, but today she hurried past without even seeing them, her only desire to put distance between herself and Eliot Buchanan as fast as possible.

CHAPTER TWO

THAT night she went to bed early, lying awake far into the night as her mind circled the incredible events of the past days. Slowly the noise and bustle of the hostel died down. After a while the traffic eased off so that the night was almost silent apart from the occasional odd sound common in old houses. The *warble-warble-warble* of an ambulance was followed by a more distant one. An accident? Perhaps. Through the thin wall she heard her neighbour moan in her sleep and then turn over, sighing gustily. The wind had dropped during the evening but it sprang up again now, whining round the corners of the building. Someone had gone to sleep with a radio on; the faint music made an eerie counterpoint to the subdued noises of people sleeping.

Tiffany had been lying with her hands behind her head, staring up at the ceiling. Now, shivering, she turned and tucked herself under the blankets. She had come to a decision. Eliot Buchanan or no Eliot Buchanan, she was not going to let the prospect of the kind of scandal he had evoked prevent her from learning to know Geoffrey Upcott. All her life she had longed for a father. Part of it was the desire to be like other children, but the other part had been a kind of groping for her roots. Now that she had at last found him she would not be frightened into running away.

There as another reason, too. Geoffrey was lonely. On his admission he did not enjoy the company of his son and daughter. It was not in Tiffany's power to turn her back on someone who needed her.

So when he rang her at the hostel the next morning and suggested that she come to dinner with him she accepted without demur and drew some of her savings out of the bank to buy herself a skirt from the shop down the road, one that she had admired in the past but been too intent on saving to buy. This, however, was an occasion and the skirt, a slim one in dark red, went well with a paler cardigan jacket her mother had bought for her. With it she wore a blouse in pinks and golds which picked up the small golden flecks in her eyes.

Her stepfather had not encouraged her to wear cosmetics but he had not forbidden them so she had always worn lipstick. Since coming to Auckland she had realised that there was a lot more to make-up than colouring her mouth. She had learned from listening to the girls who boarded with her, and had spent some time looking in the big department stores and through the fashion magazines which lay around the hostel. Marie's parting gift had been a make-up kit, small but complete. Tiffany had practised with it several times. Now she took it out and with her tongue firmly pressed in the corner of her mouth, used a blend of pink and gold shadow on her eyelids before applying mascara. Very carefully, without giving herself time to think, she touched blusher to her cheeks, then used one of the lipsticks, followed by a slick of gloss.

When she stood back and regarded herself gravely nothing much seemed to have changed except that her already large eyes looked even larger and more glowing, her cheekbones had leapt into prominence accentuating the structure of her face, and her mouth looked almost sultry.

'Goodness,' she said aloud, tilting a small square chin at the mirror before slipping into her one pair of good shoes, a plain court. She wasn't stunning or fashionable or beautiful, but at least she wouldn't look out of place.

When her father arrived she had been ready for almost ten minutes. Much of that time she had spent fuming about Eliot Buchanan and his officious arrogance. It was, she discovered, better to remain angry with him: that way she didn't feel afraid.

After considerable thought she had decided to say

nothing about the scene in the park. It would only upset Geoffrey and she didn't want to do that.

After all, she told herself firmly, it was not as though Eliot could really do anything. So her smile when she greeted her father was uncomplicated and warm and if her eyes were wary he chose not to mention it. Instead he returned her smile and kissed her cheek.

'I've made a reservation for us at a restaurant I enjoy very much,' he said. 'It's called Flamingo's, and I think you'll like it.'

'Is it very big?' Tiffany asked, not nervously but with that faint air of tension a little more apparent.

'No. Very small and very friendly. I went there one night and found that I could see into the kitchen; I watched the chef clowning around with a frying pan. It was when the English cricketers were out here and he was showing how he'd face the fast bowlers. He had the kitchen staff in gales of laughter. Me, too.'

Tiffany laughed, unconsciously relaxing. 'Was dinner long in arriving?'

'No, surprisingly quick. Now, tell me what you've been doing today.'

'Nothing much,' she said uncomfortably. 'I helped make up about fifty yards of curtains in silk velvet in the most horrendous shrimp pink. It gave me a headache to even look at it. As for living with it—ugh!'

He chuckled and began to tell her of a trick Jess the corgi had played on him that afternoon. By the time the taxi drew up outside the restaurant Tiffany was completely at ease. She looked at windows latticed in white trellis-work and felt a sudden glow of well-being. This was her father she was with and in the months to come she and he would learn to understand and appreciate each other, carefully brdging the gap the years apart had made.

Inside, the floor was tiled in black and white and a tape deck was playing a song from *Porgy and Bess*. White cloths covered tables surrounded by white wooden chairs; through an arch there was an open fire.

Flamingo's was an old house, double storeyed, with an ambience at once welcoming and casual. On each table there were candles in glass holders, flowers and little flat dishes of salt and pepper and olives.

And there was also Eliot Buchanan with a woman of terrifying sophistication who wore a black dress which fitted her slender form like a body stocking. Her expression changed from sultriness to a supercilious stare when she followed her escort's eyes and saw who had just come in.

Tiffany felt a sick thud in her stomach. Her throat tightened beneath a suddenly dry mouth. What a miserable coincidence!

Then Eliot rose and as she met his eyes she knew it was no coincidence. Somehow he had found out Geoffrey's plans and decided to mount guard on him. It would have been funny, if it hadn't been so painful.

'Well, well,' Geoffrey said, apparently pleased to see them. 'How are you, Ella, my dear? And you, Eliot. Lovely to see you both.'

By the time the greetings and the introductions were over the *maître d'hôtel* had been summoned by Eliot and they were led to another table, this one set for four. Tiffany sat down, miserably aware that she was not going to be able to eat anything under Eliot's eye or the arrogant stare that Ella Sheridan kept fixed on her.

When Geoffrey had introduced them the older woman had inclined her blonde head graciously, but there had been a nasty, knowing glint in the eyes which had mentally priced every item of clothing Tiffany wore. She spoke in a smooth, slightly too-high voice with an accent which sounded unbearably bogus.

'Are you new to Auckland, Tiffany?' she asked, seemingly with an interest not more than idle.

'Yes.' Tiffany felt a prickle of anger heat her skin.

Ella smiled sympathetically, lowering lashes over huge, hazel eyes. 'It's a big, bewildering world out there, isn't it?'

She was laying it on rather too heavily. Tiffany

returned the smile with a politeness which only just hid her antagonism.

'Well, no,' she replied coolly, 'I'm finding it very stimulating. People are fascinating but *en masse* they bear a distinct resemblance to animals in herds. Sheep, actually, in flocks. And I'm very familiar with those.'

There was a short silence during which she felt Eliot's heavy-lidded gaze on her. Then Geoffrey said something which smoothed over the hint of challenge in Tiffany's voice. Ella eagerly took her cue from him.

As they talked it became obvious that all three moved in a tight little social circle. Ella's father was a friend of Geoffrey's, had been an even closer friend of Eliot's father when he was alive and they all knew everyone whose name surfaced. Ella had only to mention that a certain name was not well known to her and immediately received a potted biography together with a caustic, short run-down on his personality, Geoffrey supplying the facts, Eliot the character-reading, and both mapping out a web of relations which eventually encompassed people Ella did know.

One big, happy family, Tiffany thought dismally, conscious that Eliot and Ella were doing it quite deliberately, excluding her from what they clearly saw as their charmed circle, making Geoffrey aware that she did not fit in.

A couple of snobs, very smooth, very beautiful, lapped by an aura of wealth and sophistication. Even their names were alike.

The meal was beautifully cooked, beautifully served. At first the food stuck in Tiffany's throat but, encouraged by a hard, fierce determination not to be cowed, she managed.

The wine helped, too. As the restaurant was not licensed none was available and Geoffrey had not bothered to bring any, explaining that he was not allowed it and Tiffany was no wine drinker.

'No?' Eliot's glance was mocking. 'But you must try some of this, Tiffany.'

'Oh, darling, why force it on her if she doesn't appreciate it?' Ella protested, smiling, her long fingers caressing his hand. She turned to Geoffrey. 'Mr Upcott, you know how dedicated Eliot is to his wine cellar. Wouldn't it be a pity for someone without a palate to drink his precious wine?'

'A good wine is the perfect place to start,' Eliot said softly. He signalled and a moment later the waitress set a glass before Tiffany then filled it with a pale liquid.

'Try it,' Eliot said. He was staring at her, his angular features totally lacking in expression.

Yet Tiffany could feel some kind of emotion reaching out to her, something that frightened her. Ella Sheridan felt it, too; she said something in a petulant voice and those rose-pink nails stroked his hand again. He ignored her, his eyes fixed on Tiffany.

Probably waiting for her to make a fool of herself, she thought grimly and lifted the glass. At exactly the same time Eliot lifted his and they drank together.

Tiffany only sipped, but the man beside her half-drained his glass.

'Well?' he asked almost roughly.

'I'll tell you when I've had some more,' Tiffany said lamely.

Ella laughed and the moment passed.

In fact, Tiffany rather liked it, but caution persuaded her to take only tiny sips, and only enough to help her food down.

'The wine is not to your liking?' Eliot's voice was smooth and bland, only a faint note of query colouring it.

'It's very nice, thank you.' Well, so it was inadequate—what did he expect? A run-down from a connoisseur when it must be too obvious that she had never tasted the stuff before? But there was no need for him to lift his brows at her gauche little reply. Less than no need for Ella to rush into speech.

'Of course, if you know nothing about . . .' she said with sweet superiority, smiling to show Geoffrey that she wasn't being nasty. Only her eyes, so unfriendly and hard, revealed that she was following Eliot's lead.

'Nothing.' Tiffany spoke with all of the composure she could summon up.

'You should learn, you know.' And Ella, who had certainly not stinted herself of wine, leaned forward and said confidentially, 'If you're going to eat at good restaurants much, it is really quite important to know about wine. Of course, if your escort knows his stuff you won't actually have to order, but you get more pleasure from wine if you know a little about it.'

'Do you think so?' Tiffany's voice was cool but without much expression. She felt that she hated Eliot Buchanan with all her heart, and Ella for following his lead, but she was careful to keep a very tight lid on her emotions. They had spoiled the evening for her; they were not going to do the same to Geoffrey.

So she listened quietly as Ella led the conversation, discoursing knowledgeably on vintages and types and soils, the inevitable French words rolling off her tongue in, presumably, a good French accent. Tiffany left her second glass of the stuff untouched; already she felt a warmth through her veins which warned her that she had had enough for the moment.

When, later, she visited the cloakroom Ella followed her, and once out of sight up the steep stairs the vivacity and wit fell away and she stared Tiffany down with an arrogant contempt which should have withered her. Possessed of that cold courage which only makes itself known when called for, Tiffany refused to respond to the older woman's provocation, until Ella said icily, 'You know, I think Geoffrey must be going senile, poor old pet. Not that I suppose he wants conversation from you, but you're practically dumb, aren't you? Still, no doubt you pay for your supper in other ways.'

Tiffany finished re-colouring her mouth. Her skin was stiff with tension but no sign of it appeared in her voice when she replied, 'What an incredibly commonplace mind you have.' And while Ella was still gaping she continued confidentially, 'I wouldn't drink any more, if I were you. You're starting to slur your words.'

'Why—you little——'

Tiffany smiled and stepped back. 'Now we learn how a lady behaves, I suppose,' she said, and watched as the other woman's hands closed in a vicious, useless gesture which must have cut her palms with those long talons.

'Get out of here,' Ella said, 'or 'I'll—I'll——'

'You're blustering. You'll do nothing. Only remember this in future. If you can't take it don't dish it out. For myself, I have manners, but some day there might wander into your circle someone who wasn't brought up nearly so well, and unless you hold your tongue you might learn all about yourself in a very ego-crushing way. It wouldn't do you any harm, of course.'

And, head held high, Tiffany walked away quickly before reaction set in and the trembling tension in her body revealed itself.

Why, she told herself as she made her way down the black stairs, you have all the makings of a first-class . . . A word hovered, but her stepfather's moral precepts were too strong. Witch, she substituted, deciding with keen satisfaction that Ella at least would think twice about attacking her so openly again.

Both men rose to their feet, the small act of courtesy emphasising Eliot's rudeness the day he had watched her walk towards him from his seat on the park bench. She met his narrowed gaze defiantly, anger and reaction lighting her eyes, her mouth held tightly to prevent it from trembling. She despised him for enlisting Ella on his side and for a moment her emotions showed only too clearly.

A muscle pulled against his jaw-bone, but she looked past him and regained control as she saw the faint anxiety in her father's face. She banished it by smiling at him; that was easy. It was much harder to keep the smile pinned on her face when Ella reappeared. Not that Ella made any open attack. She just ignored

Tiffany, totally, but both men were quick enough to pick up the tension and astute enough to guess its cause.

So the rest of the evening was uncomfortable. Tiffany was relieved when Geoffrey made a move to go but her relief rapidly became transmuted to irritation when Eliot assumed responsibility for getting them home.

'I have my car parked down the street,' he said, with cool assurance. 'Give me five minutes and I'll be back with it.'

'I'm quite capable of walking,' Geoffrey told him, his voice amused.

So they walked to the car: a different one, this one a monster of a thing which had the hallmarks of money and style and the pleasant scent of leather in the interior.

Of course Eliot drove well, reacting instantly when an idiot in a small car crashed a red light, and narrowly avoided an accident. Tiffany jumped, unable to stop herself from making a small sound of fear as the big car was swung sideways into a gap which seemed too small for it. Instantly her father touched her tightly clasped hands, his smile reassuring.

At that moment Ella Sheridan turned her head to give emphasis to her scathing remark about the driver of the other car. Her eyes fell on their linked hands. She said nothing but as she twisted back there was a certain anticipatory quality to her expression which revealed as clearly as if she had shouted it that she was looking forward to telling Eliot.

Perhaps it was that gloating look which drove home to Tiffany as nothing else had, not even Eliot's contempt, just what keeping her mother's request was going to mean. For a moment she held herself rigidly away from the man beside her, sickened. He did not speak but she knew that he understood and that he would not try to change her mind if she decided to have nothing more to do with him. He had told her that he felt he had no right to her affection or her time.

The hard, unquenchable courage which had helped her through this evening came to her aid again. Geoffrey Upcott was her father and she had every right to his company, every right to build some sort of relationship with him. Unconsciously her square chin lifted in a gesture which her mother would have recognised with resigned acceptance. Tiffany had made a decision.

But later that night, in that time between waking and sleeping, she wondered if Eliot had kissed Ella when he had delivered her home. Something the other woman had said revealed that she had her own flat; perhaps they had progressed to her bed and even now lay together in the abandonment of passion.

She pushed damp curls back from her hot brow. What did it matter to her if Ella Sheridan was Eliot's mistress? They were both thoroughly unlikeable, more than suited. But her brain would give her no rest. She imagined them naked together in a big bed, saw Eliot's face drawn with passion, and drifted off to sleep only to suffer a dream in which she replaced Ella and it was her body which he worshipped with a skill which took her into an ecstasy outside experience.

Fortunately, by the time dawn came she had almost forgotten it. The emotion she dimly recognised as an anguish of jealousy. What little of it remained she pushed into the back of her mind until it, too, was almost forgotten.

The weeks that followed were charged with a strange, waiting quality. She and her father slowly developed a routine. On fine days he came to the park or took her to lunch at one of the many small restaurants or coffee shops around Jackson's, and three or four times a week she went by taxi to his house where they spent the evenings talking and listening to music, discovering to their common pleasure that they shared an avid affection for opera and the romantic composers. Geoffrey had an enormous collection of records and a wide knowledge of music, and enjoyed the process of expanding her horizons. Books were less of an interest for Tiffany but his pleasure coaxed her into reading more than she had for years just so that she could talk about them with him. He amused himself by making up a list of works she should read if she wanted to be called educated, and because she wanted to please him she ploughed through it, finding some very enjoyable indeed, others stimulating and others difficult or boring. He laughed at her criticisms and made her justify them, so that she accused him of being a teacher at heart, and learned that he had always wanted to teach but his parents had been horrified.

'So I gave in,' he said wryly. 'The story of my life, I'm afraid. Don't allow others to live your life for you, Tiffany; not even those who love you. When you get to the end, you find that all you have achieved are other people's ambitions.'

'Nonsense,' she said robustly. 'I don't believe that you allowed yourself to be pushed around all your life. And you haven't come to the end of your life—you're not very old.'

'I'm over sixty, and don't try to tell me that you don't consider me aged, because I can remember how I viewed anyone over thirty when I was twenty-two.'

'Well, so what? Plenty of people live to be ninety. Why don't you go along to the local school and offer to hear children read? Or——'

He laughed and said something about her forthright character and the subject lapsed, but afterwards Tiffany remembered it, and wept.

She learnt a lot those evenings. Talking with a clever, worldly man broadened her knowledge but it was the intangibles he passed on to her which matured her. Unconsciously she absorbed attitudes and standards; she did not realise, then or later, that he was giving her the confidence to be herself. Not until long after did she appreciate that he had deliberately set out to do so.

Occasionally they went out to dinner, but usually their evenings were spent quietly and alone at his house.

The first time Eliot came Tiffany was ill-at-ease, but it seemed that he had no intention of carrying on open warfare in his uncle's presence. He spent most of the evening talking to Geoffrey but she listened, finding to her surprise that she enjoyed the stimulating meeting of two good brains.

At eleven o'clock he offered to take Tiffany back to the hostel. When Geoffrey refused for her Eliot lifted his brows but said nothing and what could have been an awkward moment passed by.

'He's been in Australia on business. I'm glad he's back,' Geoffrey said after he had closed the door on his departing nephew. 'I enjoy talking to him. He's very like his father, every bit as clever, but he has a keen sense of humour which Philip missed out on.' He paused as though inviting comment, but when Tiffany said nothing he resumed, 'You don't like him, do you?'

'Not much,' she said uncomfortably. 'He's a bit intimidating.'

Geoffrey chuckled. 'Well, you don't show it. He comes to see me at least once a week. Beneath that glittering air of command there's a kind heart.'

Perhaps, but certainly not where Tiffany was concerned. Her hope that Eliot's night for being kind didn't coincide with her visits again was without success, for the one night he visited each week became two, even, on occasions, three.

There was nothing Tiffany could do about it. Once she had mentioned rather wistfully to her father that she hadly ever saw him by herself now, and he had said something so non-committal that she realised he wanted it this way. Or, if not wanted, at least accepted it.

So she forced herself to ignore the tension which Eliot brought with him. Her efforts were made easier by the fact that his attitude to her never wavered. He treated her like a young cousin, and only the cold condemnation in his eyes revealed his true opinion.

What Geoffrey thought of the situation she didn't know. He certainly enjoyed their occasional arguments, listening with an air of amused interest to the swift exchange of views. Not that Eliot spoke much to her. With the insight gained from his affection for his uncle, he knew exactly the sort of things Geoffrey wanted to hear and kept him interested with accounts of deals in the city and the inside story on any political news of the day. As well, he relayed gossip about people known to both of them, mostly financial. Nothing was said that a fifteen-year-old girl couldn't have listened to, but sometimes, when she was in the tiny kitchen making coffee, Tiffany heard a different sort of laughter and realised that some of the gossip was of a more personal sort.

That Geoffrey enjoyed these sessions was obvious, so Tiffany endured them. Then one Sunday night, just after she had come back from church, she was called to the telephone. It was Eliot.

'Geoffrey died an hour ago,' he said without preamble.

Somehow Tiffany wasn't surprised. Shaken and grieved, yes, but subconsciously she must have been expecting it. She felt anguish, keen and sharp as the blade of a knife, and her free hand pressed against her heart.

'Tiffany?' He was impatient; she could hear it in his voice.

'Yes, I'm here,' she said dully. 'What did he die of?'

'A heart attack. He was warned not to over-exert himself. Let's hope you didn't kill him.'

She knew why he was so brutal. For an unguarded moment his superb control had slipped and she heard raw pain and grief in the deep voice.

'When is the funeral?' she asked.

'Tuesday morning. Which brings me to my reason for ringing. You are definitely not welcome at the funeral.'

'Of course not,' she said tonelessly.

The telephone booth had been repainted not very long before in a particularly repellant shade of yellow. Someone—some several ones—had already scribbled numbers on the wall and the paint was that special institutional sort which dries with a smeary, slightly grubby surface. Tiffany stood staring at one of the numbers, as the digits arranged and rearranged themselves in front of her. She was, she realised, crying. Not sobbing; it was just silent tears which ran down her face.

'However,' Eliot's merciless voice went on, 'you are a beneficiary in his will. I'll pick you up Wednesday lunchtime.

'You needn't bother.' She swallowed hard, trying to get rid of the hard lump in her chest. 'I shan't come . . .'

'Oh, spare me the big renunciation scene,' he interrupted, weariness flattening his voice. 'Just be there. We can discuss it then.'

The telephone clicked, and Tiffany stood stupidly with the useless receiver pressed to her ear. A girl came past. She stopped and looked curiously at Tiffany.

'Bad news?' she asked.

Tiffany realised how she must look. 'Yes,' she said simply and finally hung up.

'Look,' the girl began, but Tiffany shook her head.

'I'll be all right,' she said. 'It was—not unexpected.'

'Do you want a cup of tea or something?'

She was trying to help and Tiffany warmed to her but she said, 'No, I'll go and lie down for a while. It's not—that big a deal.'

The girl nodded and left her but she must have been worried about her for about half an hour later the matron, a nice, middle-aged woman, came to her room and asked if there was anything she could do.

'No thank you.' Tiffany had been lying dry-eyed on her bed. 'I am—I'm fine now.'

'A death?'

'Yes.'

'A relative?'

'Yes.' Just my father, she thought wearily as the woman offered condolences. My father who only knew me for such a short time.

News travels fast in any sort of institution. Tiffany was touched when the other boarders offered their sympathy, most of them awkwardly, as if death had not yet touched them and they had no idea how to deal with it. But their condolences warmed her, made her feel less alone. She wrote to her mother, mentioning his death as though he had just been an old man she met in the park. How would Marie feel? Tiffany could not visualise herself in such a situation.

The death announcement was in the newspaper, as was a short article on Geoffrey's career. She clipped them both out and went to the cemetery stipulated in the announcement. There, amidst the impressive array of wreaths and flowers on the unmade grave, she put a small posy of flowers without a card. Tears came again, but she had cried out most of her grief and after a few minutes she regained command of herself and made the wearisome bus journey back to the hostel.

When she came out from work on Wednesday, Eliot was sitting in his car just up the street. This time he got out as she approached, his expression grim as he scanned her face. She wasn't looking her best; her olive skin made it difficult for her to lose colour attractively. She knew that she was sallow and tired, but she gave him look for look, seeing evidence of his affection for his uncle in the pronounced jut of bone beneath skin which looked too tightly stretched. All the luminescence had faded from his eyes; they were dark and cold.

But he was still incredibly charismatic, that magnetic aura as pronounced as ever. As he handed her into the front seat two girls coming towards them looked enviously, first at the opulence of the Lotus and then at the man, and into both faces flashed an immediate sensual awareness.

'I've booked lunch for us,' he said as he put the car into motion.

Tiffany looked down at her clothes. Neat, but definitely not suited for lunch at a restaurant. She made no protest. No doubt he wanted to put her at a disadvantage. Well, he would find out that she refused to be terrorised by his dislike.

The restaurant was elegant, he clearly well-known there, and the waiters too well-trained to betray their surprise at his companion. Stoically Tiffany perused the menu, decided on an omelette which she knew she wasn't going to be able to eat and refused wine.

Then, when the waiters had done their thing, Eliot said curtly, 'Geoffrey set up a trust fund for you. He also left you the house and his grandmother's jewllery.'

The sneer in his voice barely impinged. She smiled, glad that her father had been sentimental enough to leave her something which had belonged to that first Tifaine; he had told her a lot about the tough little woman who had been the only person to love him when he was a child.

'Pleased?' Eliot taunted, dropping his voice. 'Not too soon, Tiffany. Geoffrey's children are going to contest the will and if their case is not upheld then I am your sole trustee. In effect, I control exactly what you get from it. Which will be as little as I can make it. And his grandmother's jewellery is only a few modest bits and pieces, together hardly the value of a single decent piece.'

The sprinkling of gold flakes in her eyes blazed up, engulfing them. 'Is that all you have to tell me?' she asked.

'Wasn't it as much as you hoped for? Yes, that's your share of the loot.'

'Then I'm sure you won't mind if I leave you,' she said politely and made to rise.

'No.' Too quickly for her to avoid it his hand caught her wrist, caught and clamped on to the strong, delicate bones with cruel force.

Between his teeth he continued, 'At the moment no one realises what I'm doing. That fat lady over there thinks I'm holding your hand. But you make one move to leave this table and I'll give the whole lot something to talk about for months.'

For a moment she wavered. He was elegant in a dark suit, businessman's attire, conventional from the polished shoes to his smooth dark hair. Men dressed like that didn't do the things his eyes were threatening her with. Yet she subsided back into her chair, her eyes dilated, and faintly heard her breath escape from her lungs in a long sigh.

'Good girl,' he said. Again the words—even the tone—were bland, conventional, yet it was a pirate who stared her down, his expression icily purposeful as though it would give him intense satisfaction to humiliate her publicly.

After that she refused to make more than monosyllabic replies to him, but he forced her to stay there while he ate and she pushed the omelette around her plate.

'The fat lady is now quite convinced that we are lovers who have quarrelled,' he taunted. 'No doubt she's sighing romantically over the pleasures of making up.'

Tiffany's eyes ran insolently over his form, then she looked down at herself. 'Lovers?' she asked politely. 'Do—men like you—take women like me as lovers?'

She had touched a nerve—touched it? She had jabbed it with a spear! He actually went pale beneath the tan which showed no signs of fading and as she watched, fascinated, his mouth pulled into a thin, cruel line.

At that moment the *maître d'hôtel* came regally by and stopped to ask if everything had been satisfactory. It gave Tiffany great pleasure to see Eliot visibly make himself control his anger before he replied in the affirmative. As soon as they were alone he stood up and swept her out of the place, his fingers cruelly tight on her arm.

Once in the car he said nothing except, 'I'll be in touch with you,' before he drove off.

Tiffany went back to work feeling as though she had spent the lunch hour picking her way across a minefield. Terrifying, yet the surge of adrenalin he produced in her had banished some of her grief.

It was on her way home that she began to worry over Jess's well-being. Geoffrey had told her that his children—his *other* children—did not like dogs. Surely they would have found somewhere for the little corgi to go? Yet before she had consciously made a decision to go and see for herself what had happened she found herself on a bus heading for Remuera. One of Geoffrey's neighbours in the town houses, an elderly widow whose name she couldn't remember, was a dog lover and should know where Jess was.

She did. In fact, she had her.

'Well, when they were going to have her put down, I had to do something,' she told Tiffany defensively. 'The moving men left the gate open and she was running around, poor little thing, crying for Mr Upcott, so I just brought her in here and—kept her.'

Tiffany pushed her hand through her hair. 'What—I'm sorry, but what moving men?' she asked.

'My dear, they were here the morning after Mr Upcott died. I went out—you hear such stories about how bold thieves are nowadays—but *they* were there, so it was all right. But it was barely decent!'

'They?'

'His children. Mrs March and Colin Upcott. They took everything away. And didn't bother to clean up after themselves either. I've swept it out——'

'Have you a key, Mrs Crowe?' Tiffany bent down to stroke Jess's head, her fingers trembling as they caressed the foxy ears. Jess was grieving, eyes no longer bright and alert and full of interested delight in her world.

The older woman looked self-conscious. 'Yes, I have, as it happens. Mr Upcott gave me one when he had to go away not so long ago and I looked after Jess. She was happier sleeping in her own home. I meant to give it back, but ... And now I have to go to my daughter's at Gisborne, and I simply don't know what to do about Jess. I don't suppose you could ...?'

Tiffany felt the small warm body pressed against her

legs. She was angry, with a deep, bitter anger which gave her the courage to say, 'Yes, I'll take her. In fact, if you give me the key, I'll move in next door.' She managed to sound casual as she said, 'Mr Upcott left it to me.'

Mrs Crowe wouldn't have been human if she hadn't been curious but she hid it manfully, though she was reluctant to let Tiffany have the key. It was understandable, of course. In the end Tiffany rang Eliot's home address and, after speaking to someone whose voice was like enough to his to be his mother, got him.

'What do you want?'

Well, what had she expected? Concisely she explained what had happened and her decision to move into Geoffrey's house. She didn't say anything about the indecent removal of his furniture; probably he knew of it and approved.

'You have no legal title until his will is probated,' he said abruptly when she had finished.

'I don't care. I'm moving in. If they contest and win then I'll move out, but by then I'll have found a home for Jess.'

There was a pause. She could imagine him frowning slightly, his expression abstracted, as he decided what to do. Finally he said, 'All right, I'll take the responsibility. Just make sure that you've enough money to pay the rent which will be demanded from you if they win their case.'

'Charming couple, aren't they,' she said lightly. 'No doubt encouraged by you.'

'Disappointed, Tiffany? What——' From somewhere in the background came a woman's voice, not the pleasant tones of his mother but the distinctive, drawling voice of Ella Sheridan.

Eliot laughed and said, 'I'll be with you in a minute, darling.'

Before he could finish whatever insult he had intended to fling at her she said, 'Could you please explain to Mrs Crowe that it's all above-board then?'

'Oh, very well.'

He did, so that the older woman was completely won over, effusing over him even after Tiffany felt she had made it quite clear that she was tired of the subject.

She moved in over the weekend, having raided her savings to buy herself the cheapest bed she could find and enough bedclothes to ensure that she didn't freeze. There was absolutely nothing in the house except a heap of old rags which had been left in the garage and the built-in shelves they hadn't been able to take. Even the gardening tools were gone. But she had a bed and two towels, and on Saturday morning she bought a knife and a fork and a spoon, a few foodstuffs and enough crockery so that she didn't have to eat off the bench. As well as a bone for Jess.

Nothing else, no chairs or table, not even curtains, for they, too, had gone. Fortunately the sitting room looked out on to the high walled courtyard.

'As for the bedroom. I'll just have to undress in the dark' Tiffany told Jess.

All in all, it had been quite a weekend.

On Sunday afternoon Tiffany snapped the leash on Jess and said, 'Come on, sweetie, let's go for a long, long walk to blow the cobwebs away.'

Jess signified her approval by barking and jumping up; she still pined for Geoffrey, only forgetting him when she was out of the house. The day before Tiffany had taken her to the little park down the road but today she decided to explore this part of the suburb.

Although the sky looked ominous as they left, it soon cleared. The cool, crisp air was so refreshing, so calming after the tension of the week past, that Tiffany neglected to keep a close watch on the weather.

They were only half a mile from home on the way back when the rain began to fall, but there was no way they were going to get anything other than saturated. It pelted down, cold and nasty, each drop hitting with force so that before she had run more than fifty yards Tiffany was soaked to the skin. With her thick coat Jess was a little better off, but by the time they were half-way home both animal and human were shivering and miserable.

When the car drew to a halt beside them Tiffany couldn't help her hopeful look. Back home—but this was not back home. Then she stiffened, for it was Eliot who opened the door.

'Get in!' he ordered.

She shook her head. 'I'm soaking, and so is Jess. It's not much further now.'

'*Get in*. Or I'll make you.'

He looked angry enough to do just that. Shivering, not entirely with the cold, Tiffany climbed in, holding Jess in her arms in an attempt to stop her from shaking herself all over the beautiful interior.

'You needn't——' she began, only to have him interrupt savagely,

'Shut up, will you.'

And that was the sum total of their conversation until he drew up outside the garage.

Then he said, 'Open the door,' and when she gaped at him, 'You're wet, I'm not. And find me a rag so that I can mop up, will you.'

'Look, you didn't have to pick us up,' she began, only to be interrupted again.

This time he spoke between his teeth. 'Just do as you're told. And fast.'

She hurried, grabbing an old towel from the rags Geoffrey's children had left behind. Inside the garage it was dark, so she switched on the fluorescent light and watched as Jess shook herself with great enthusiasm, luckily choosing the empty half of the garage.

'Get into some dry clothes,' Eliot ordered harshly.

'Jess——'

'I'll do the bloody dog. Get into some dry clothes. And have a shower before you do it.'

When she stared mute defiance he threatened, 'Or I'll put you in one myself.'

She fled, shedding her jersey and shoes in the laundry

before running up the stairs as if she was being pursued by the Furies. Or one of them.

Twenty minutes later when she came downstairs her composure was almost fully restored. She had chosen to wear a deep garnet-red corduroy skirt and a prim woollen shirt of the same colour with long sleeves and a big collar which almost covered the slight contours of her breasts. Damp curls clustered thickly around her head, making her look no more than sixteen.

CHAPTER THREE

JESS was lying on the mat by the glass sliding door, watching Eliot with an interest which made it clear how much she missed her man. She had been thoroughly dried and was wearing the smug look of a dog who has just had an illicit snack.

Eliot stared out at the rain-drenched courtyard. He looked very big and very austere, the clean autocratic lines of his face harsh against the dull greyness of the day outside. One lamp was on. The golden light gleamed over the tanned skin, darkening his eyes, emphasising the arrogant bone structure which gave his face its strength and a beauty far removed from handsomeness. He was the most explosively attractive man she had ever seen, his whole body poised and superbly balanced, alive with an electric sexuality. He terrified her.

She had made no noise but his head whipped around and his eyes found hers. 'I've made coffee,' he said. 'Get it inside you.'

'Thank you.'

'You couldn't wait to get rid of every memory of Geoffrey,' he said savagely. 'I did warn you, if you remember, that taking a lover as old as him was hardly likely to be an ecstatic experience. Still, I'd have thought that gratitude for his generosity would have prevented such a clean sweep. There were some quite good pieces here—no doubt you got a fair price for them. I hope you didn't just contact an ordinary second hand dealer.'

The insulted need no underlining. Tiffany cradled the coffee mug in her hands as she answered, 'When I arrived here everything was gone. Mrs Crowe next door told me that a removal van arrived the day after Geoffrey's death. I thought you must have organised it.'

He actually looked outraged for a moment before his lashes hid his thought. 'I certainly did not,' he said with curt emphasis.

Incredibly enough she believed him. 'His children, then.'

'Legally they were within their rights. This house was left to you; he did not mention the contents.'

She nodded, feeling sick. 'It's just as well Mrs Crowe was there and took Jess in. Apparently they were going to have her put down.'

The mention of her name brought Jess's head around. She snorted before rolling over on to her back.

'Not everyone likes dogs,' Eliot said, almost defensively.

'Of course not.' She finished the coffee, burning her tongue in the process, and asked politely. 'Would you like something to drink? I'm afraid there's only coffee or tea.'

'No. And this is ridiculous.' He cast a sweeping look around the bare room. 'I'll advance you a sum tomorrow to cover your immediate expenses. Have you left your job?'

'No, of course not.' She saw his glance rest on Jess and continued, 'She's all right during the day. When Mrs Crowe comes back from her holiday she said that she'd have her. Until then she seems quite happy inside.'

'Oh, to hell with the damned dog!' He spoke impatiently, anger tightening his mouth. 'You know, Tiffany, I still haven't decided whether you're as naïve as you seem to be or are putting on an elaborate charade.'

'I thought that you had made up your mind,' she retorted. 'So quickly, too. Within minutes of meeting me. Now there's a man who makes rapid decisions, I thought, when you favoured me with your reading of my character a week or so later. One look and that was it, all my secrets laid bare before your all-seeing eyes.'

Her sarcasm was juvenile and she hadn't expected it

to hit home. But the angry colour deepened along his cheekbones and he said silkily as he came towards her, 'You should watch your tongue, Tiffany, or it just might get you into trouble. Like this . . .'

The coffee mug was taken from her hands and placed carefully on the bench. Frozen in a kind of suspension of belief she stood rigidly as he straightened up and took her hands in his, jerking her towards him. When his intention became clear she tried to twist away. His grip held firm even when her struggles became desperate. Jess snapped to her feet and growled.

'Quiet!' The single word kept the dog still but Tiffany muttered, '*No*—no—I didn't.'

'Yes, you did,' he said quite calmly, holding her still against him by the simple expedient of grabbing a handful of hair and twisting it until the pain kept her quiescent. He smiled into her frightened face and lowered his head so that when he spoke the words were little explosions against Tiffany's suddenly sensitised lips.

'You were as provocative as you know how to be,' he said blandly. 'Now you must take the consequences.'

Tiffany was not a complete innocent. She had been kissed quite often. She had read of kisses being used as a punishment but she had never expected to be forced back into line by this method.

Her eyes stretched wide open as his mouth dropped the last fraction on to hers; his dark face blurred, became indistinct. She expected him to hurt her but his lips moved gently, softly as though he was tasting her. In fact, if it wasn't for the hands which tangled her hair so cruelly she might have believed that he was enjoying what he was doing.

When he lifted his head and looked into her eyes she felt a chill of emptiness.

'Nice,' he said with cool deliberation. 'But not enough.'

His eyes blazed into flames as his mouth came down again, forcing her lips apart so that he could explore the depths of her mouth in a kiss so unlike any other she had ever received that she thought she might faint. Indeed, her knees did buckle. He made a noise deep in his throat and shifted one arm so that it supported her. His mouth burned down the stretched arc of her throat.

The weakness in her limbs spread until she was trembling. Deep inside her strange sensations sprang into life; they flamed fiercely, heating her blood so that a flush ran like fire across her skin.

Without volition her hands came up to grip his shoulders, then slid beneath his arms to link behind his back, holding him close. He muttered something against her throat and released her hair, stroking slowly, languorously, down the length of her body until she was pressed against his taut strength of muscle and bone. The evidence of his arousal made her gasp and flinch away but he muttered, 'No, not yet, my lovely,' and kissed her again, a hard, thrusting kiss which released some hidden spring inside her, opening her mind to the full realisation of her own sexuality.

Later she would be astounded that it was Eliot Buchanan who had the power to bring her body to this singing, heated life but now the sensations which burnt through her veins and flesh held her silent.

'Don't struggle,' he whispered thickly. 'You want this as much as I do.'

But she could feel the barely leashed passion which lay behind the mask of control and fear jerked her free from his arms. One hand pressed against her hot, swollen mouth; above it her eyes were dazed, the pupils enormous in her flushed face.

'You're an expert at projecting injured innocence,' Eliot said on a sneer. 'Was that what turned Geoffrey on? It doesn't do much for me so you can drop the pose.'

Tiffany barely heard him. Her whole being had drawn in on itself; she was very close to a state of shock and quite incapable of anything like a logical response. In all her romantic dreams, and she had had quite a few, she had never expected that she could respond like that to a man's kiss. He had touched her and her body had sung like a harp string tuned only to one man's hand. How could she hate him yet be wracked by sensations so piercingly exciting that even now her pulse accelerated at the remembrance of them?

It was her first experience of desire and now that it was over she was both repelled and terrified at her vulnerability. Did he know that she ached for him?

He was still watching her, the heavy eyelids covering all but a fraction of his eyes so that she could not tell what he was thinking. Beneath the tan he was pale and his mouth had set into a hard, thin line. She cursed her lack of experience because it meant that she could get no clues about how the unexpected embrace had affected him.

That he was angry she was almost convinced but even as she stared he turned away, saying harshly, 'Oh, stop looking so appalled. I can promise you that it won't happen again.'

'I'm glad.' Her mouth was stiff, forming words she didn't recognise. 'Would you mind going? I'm not—I don't——'

'Are you all right?' The words seemed to be forced from him; even as he said them he turned away with an expressive gesture of disgust. 'Of course you are. That's an excellent disguise you wear, Tiffany: such big, horrified eyes and quivering lips and that superb expression of complete innocence. You should have quite a future ahead of you pandering to jaded old men who like to fantasise about willing, nubile little virgins.'

'You are despicable,' she breathed. 'Get out of here!'

When he had gone she sank down on to the floor, hiding the fierce, hot tears with her hands. He was vile, vile, accusing her of a kind of depravity which made her sick when she thought of it. Innocence was all very well, she thought bitterly, but it didn't prepare you for people like Eliot Buchanan who was so cynical that he couldn't admit that there might be an interpretation other than his of the relationship between his uncle and Tiffany.

He was hateful. So why had she responded to his kiss with such fierce exultation? Sexual chemistry—it was as simple as that. Somehow he had the power to arouse her in the most basic way so that she desired him in spite of the warnings her brain despatched. It was not one-sided, either. Like her, he had tried to hide it, but from that first meeting there had been that awareness, the strange threads of sensual tension which spun between them making a net which could only destroy her if she allowed herself to be caught in it.

As Tiffany groaned Jess came over and sat down in front of her, her sharp little face lifted with some anxiety. Wiping the tears away with the back of her hand Tiffany said wearily, 'I am a fool, Jess. A naïve idiot.'

Jess seemed to agree but she subsided back into her usual position, resting her nose on her paws, watching the pale face above her. It pleased Tiffany to think that the dog somehow sensed her turmoil and was offering comfort.

For comfort was definitely what she needed. Had she been at home she would have tried to work through her bewilderment by talking to her mother. Marie must have felt this same kind of attraction or she would not have compromised her ideals by becoming her employer's lover. Geoffrey had said that their affair was caused by mutual loneliness but Tiffany could not believe that. Marie must have loved him. Or had she been caught in the same dark enchantment which was hovering over her daughter now?

Once, she had told Tiffany that attraction was an important part of adult love but by itself was a falsely glamorous illusion which could lead to heartbreak and despair. Tiffany had listened but not appreciated what her mother was saying; now she understood.

Sighing, she stroked a finger through Jess's fine ginger fur. She did not want to think of the humiliating

minutes she had spent in Eliot's arms but her basic
strength forced her to accept that weakness. If he had
done more than kiss her, if he had caressed her as her
body had so ardently desired, then she would have had
great difficulty in resisting him.

The lure of the forbidden, she thought, appalled at
her behaviour. Surely it was impossible that one man, a
man she actually disliked who felt nothing but
contempt for her, should be able to overturn every
principle, every restraint her somewhat rigid upbringing
had been based on. Apparently not, and that meant
that she would have to make certain that she never saw
him alone again.

The decision made, she fought to rid her mind—and
her body—of his influence.

Two days later a cheque arrived in the mail. In formal
lawyer's language the accompanying letter told her that
it was an advance on the amount she was due to receive
from Geoffrey's will. It was signed by Eliot.

The sheet of paper trembled in her hand. The
signature was black and legible, not ostentatious or
dramatic but a definite indication of his character,
harsh against the thick white paper. Attached to it was
a cheque made out for more money than she had ever
thought to see.

With it she bought the sewing machine she coveted, a
chair and table, some more towels and a big meaty
bone for Jess. The rest went into her bank account.

That night she sat up late, planning. What she had in
mind would take nerve and determination but it would
be much more satisfying than her present job. Also it
would keep her too busy to grieve—or to recall those
maddened minutes she had spent being kissed by Eliot
Buchanan.

The next day she bought fabric and ribbons and laces
and other sewing necessities, after consultation with the
most accessible of the decorators at Jackson's, Sylvia
Cloud, who had been quite interested when Tiffany had

screwed up her courage several notches to knock on her office door.

'Well, I wish you luck,' Mrs Cloud had said after Tiffany explained her plans. 'There is certainly an opening for a creative new approach to table linens and cushions, and I agree, the selection here is pretty basic. But you won't be able to earn your living at it for a while, you know. If your stuff catches on then the sky's the limit as long as you keep producing a new and exciting product.'

Within a week Tiffany produced her first samples, table mats and napkins, delicately machine appliquéd, and several cushion covers in the shape of fruit and vegetables.

Mrs Cloud checked them over carefully. 'Yes,' she said after several nerve-stretching minutes. 'These are extremely attractive. Well made, too.'

She called in the buyer, who looked at Tiffany with vague recognition before checking her sample with a much keener eye. 'Well,' he said at last. 'Yes, I like them.' He looked at Mrs Cloud. A silent message passed between them. Turning briskly to an immensely relieved Tiffany he went on, 'How many can you supply?'

'As many as you want,' Tiffany returned promptly, and Mrs Cloud laughed and he grinned.

'Right, let's get down to business,' he said.

Half an hour later Tiffany walked out into the street feeling as though she was walking on air. What her stepfather had always thought a somewhat suspect talent looked as though it might be going to earn her living. The buyer hadn't exactly been madly optimistic but he had liked what he had seen.

Just before she left for home that evening Mrs Cloud appeared in the grim little passageway outside the workroom.

'Ah, there you are,' she said, smiling. 'We've sold two of your samples already and one woman wants another set of the strawberry ones. Can do?'

Tiffany laughed. 'Oh, can do, indeed,' she said.

The euphoria lasted until well after she had taken Jess for a quick run in the park, eaten a snack dinner and settled down to sew. By the time she had finished it was late and her eyes were stinging but the strawberry mats and napkins were finished and so was another set, kowhai flowers this time, which she planned to show to a shop in her local shopping centre specialising in linens of all sorts.

What followed were the most hectic weeks she had ever endured. Incredibly it seemed that her wares were an overnight success so that she had to spend every spare minute sewing to keep up with the demand. She was able to banish Eliot's image very successfully from her mind, at least while she was awake. What happened while she slept was another story, but fortunately dreams fade quickly from the conscious mind and if anyone had asked her she would have said, and almost believed it to be true, that she never thought of him.

One day in the depths of winter Mrs Cloud said, 'Have you thought of doing this full time?'

'Well, yes, but I don't know whether to or not. It's a big step.'

'I think you could, you know. You have imagination and a creative flair, your finishing is excellent and we have people clamouring for your stuff. Mind you, I'm not promising that you'll make a fortune, but so far the demand is holding—actually, it's increasing. So if I were you I'd think seriously about giving up your job and finding yourself an accountant; you'll be kept too busy to want to be doing the books yourself.'

That night Tiffany did no sewing. Instead she sat on her chair and thought seriously and long about leaving behind the security her job represented. Deep down she was afraid, but with the fear there was also exhilaration and excitement, so that she said to Jess, 'I think I must be a gambler,' and laughed when the dog rolled over on to her back.

The next day she handed in her notice, and the

ensuing fortnight was spent in ever-increasing doubts as to whether she had done the right thing. On her last day she was touched when the other seamstresses gave her a morning tea party and a small gift and she thanked them with a husky voice.

They seemed pleased with her reaction and wished her good luck, repeating their good wishes as they left for home that night.

Mrs Cloud did the same, adding, 'If you get into strife feel free to come and see me.'

Touched again Tiffany smiled mistily at her. 'Thank you,' she said.

'I come from the country too,' Mrs Cloud told her drily, 'and I fought and bled and worked for where I've got, such as it is. I like to think I can pick those people who are going to make it; I think you've got that extra something that will take you a long way. Just steer clear of the men until you get where you're going.'

A certain bitter note in the decorator's voice made Tiffany deduce that Mrs Cloud had suffered a bad marriage. Or perhaps a bad relationship, as they seemed to be the thing at the moment.

She wondered if she would ever acquire the sort of worldliness which accepted 'relationships', meaningful or otherwise, and the affairs that people like Eliot indulged in, as the norm. The idea filled her with a fastidious disgust. From the few things Geoffrey had said about Eliot's private life she gathered that he was not promiscuous, but no celibate either.

'He is a virile man,' Geoffrey had said quietly when her expressive face showed her emotions. 'And if no one gets hurt . . .'

It had been a touchy subject and they had not known each other well enough to discuss it further. But remembering her mother's assertions about the place of romance in marriage, Tiffany couldn't help but wonder if there ever were love affairs in which no one was hurt!

It was strange to be able to stay at home. Tiffany was determined to be professional about it so each weekday she sat down to the sewing machine at eight-thirty, not finishing until four-thirty.

The days passed quickly, if in somewhat depressing loneliness. Now that she only had Jess to communicate with she found herself missing her family more than she had when she first left home. Geoffrey, too; she had known him for such a little time yet her grief was very real and deep.

And she, like Jess, looked for a masculine presence. It was only because Eliot was—stimulating, with his abrasive, electric personality and his quick brain, she told herself severely.

'I must make the effort to go out,' she said to Jess, who wagged her ridiculous excuse for a tail and yawned.

'It's all very well for you,' Tiffany complained severely. 'You're recovering nicely, but I need a little social contact now and then.'

Sighing, she looked around the room. Since the arrival of the cheque she had carefully bought second-hand furniture, an old sofa which she had loose-covered in a pretty Designers' Guild print in her favourite shades of rose-pink and green and grey to blend in with the deep green carpet. An old wooden chest served as storage and gave her somewhere to put a vase of jonquils from the garden and her coffee mug. In answer to her request her mother had begun to send up her books. They were a little forlorn in the built-in bookshelves, but she had discovered an excellent second-hand bookshop in a mall in Newmarket and was busy augmenting her collection so that the shelves no longer appeared desolate.

For the wide wall opposite the windows she had made a wall-hanging, water lilies on a pond, which was softly romantic. Even to her critical eyes it looked good. Upstairs the only furniture was a second-hand chest of drawers and her bed, but that was now covered by a duvet. She had chosen a rose-pink material with a green geometric design to hide the utilitarian duvet.

The house was no longer bare and echoing, even though there were still no curtains and she possessed only one coffee mug and one setting of china, and that the cheapest she could find that she liked. In the pantry there was a small store of basic foods and she shopped carefully so that her food cost as little as possible, for although she was selling everything she could make she knew there was nothing so fickle as fashion. Sometimes at night she woke, terrified, her brain whirling with inchoate fears, seeing herself bankrupt and forced to go to her stepfather for help. He would help her, of course, but he would make sure she knew of his disapproval.

The rest of the cheque Eliot had sent had stayed in the bank. It gave her some reassurance, but she had determined not to make use of any more of her father's legacy. It was her reserve, her standby, not to be touched. She had no idea how long it took to get probate for a will and even less how much her share of Geoffrey's estate would come to. It would not be much.

A few days after she had received the cheque, another letter had arrived from Eliot's office, written by a person she did not know. It explained that the enclosed package had been found in Geoffrey's papers and, in accordance with the instructions on the envelope, had been sent to her. There were no signs that it had been tampered with so the contents were known only to her.

It was a letter in which he claimed her for his daughter. He wrote that he would have liked to give her the proportion of his estate to which she was entitled but that if he had his other children would almost certainly contest the will. If that happened, and for her mother's sake she refused to divulge their relationship, his legitimate children would probably win.

He must have known how little time he had left. He thanked her for the pleasure she had given him in their times together, and ended with a request, rather drily delivered, that she trust Eliot.

'I know that you don't like him,' the letter ended, 'and he certainly believes that he dislikes you. But he is completely trustworthy and will do his best as your trustee. Rely on him, but do not tell him who you are until you think the time is right. You will know when that is.'

An odd request to make. During the subsequent days Tiffany had wondered often what Geoffrey meant. Now she pondered the words again, angry with herself because she couldn't banish Eliot's image from her brain. It just wasn't fair for a man to have such impact that she could see him in spite of her efforts to keep him out of her thoughts. Close her eyes and there he was, the lean elegance which belied his great strength, the brilliance of his eyes, so at odds with the tanned skin and dark hair. He wasn't even conventionally handsome!

But of course he didn't need to be. The arrogant, fine-boned features were impressed with a power which surpassed mere good looks and he possessed a sexual chemistry which was as potent as a drug.

She was sitting dreamily trying to work out just how he fascinated the senses when the doorbell shrilled in quick sharp spurts of sound, impatient through the quiet house. Tiffany shrank into her chair, as terrified as if her imagination had conjured him for her from thin air. Common sense set her on her feet but she had to compose her features into a completely dead-pan expression, for an idiotic upspring of joy had fountained through her, setting her pulses racing and bringing to life the tiny gold lights in her eyes.

'May I come in?' Eliot asked curtly after one keen appraising look.

She stood back, unaware that until then she had been blocking the way. Silently she led the way across the sitting room.

'Sit down,' she said, wincing as her head gave a sudden, painful jolt.

'What's the matter?'

She pushed a hand against her sore neck muscles, before gesturing towards the sofa. 'Nothing. I've just got a thick head.'

He had been watching her with far too much interest, but at her words his head turned to where the bedcover she had been making spilled across the bench in a flood of black and gold.

'You shouldn't be sewing,' he said, dark brows drawn together in a straight line. 'Sit down and I'll make you a cup of tea. Have you taken anything for the headache?'

'All I need is a little fresh air,' she objected, astonished at how sweet it was to be fussed over even in such an impersonal way. 'And I don't need tea or coffee either. What do you want?'

Ignoring her churlishness he set the briefcase on to the chest. Tiffany watched as his lean hands opened it, moved deftly to extract several sheets of paper.

'This is a copy of the valuation of the jewellery you were left in Geoffrey's will,' he told her without expression.

'But I thought——'

'You thought?'

'I thought that you couldn't do anything with it until—well, until Geoffrey's children decided whether or not to contest,' she said after a pause.

'They're not going to contest. That being so there is no reason—no *legal* reason, why you should not take delivery of the jewellery.'

He ran a contemptuous glance the length of the slender body held so rigidly away from him. His taunt about her lack of moral right to the jewels had registered but she was determined not to let him see how much it hurt.

She hid the quick colour which ran up through her translucent skin by saying, 'I see. Thank you.' Her eyes rested contemplatively on the sheets of paper in his hand.

Her quietness seemed to irritate him for he asked savagely, 'Do you want them checked by another jeweller? I can assure you that I'm not in the habit of cheating clients, but if you'd feel happier, by all means get someone else.'

'Oh, I believe you,' she said huskily, holding his glance. 'That you're not in the habit of cheating, I mean. But I'm sure you'd make an exception to that rule for me.'

The autocratic features sharpened into anger. 'No, not for you,' he said, contempt running in a dark note through his voice. 'No exceptions for you, Tiffany. Never.'

It was a threat, delivered with a menacing promise which should have terrified her. But the dark aloofness of her glance didn't waver. If she once let him see how intimidated she was by his ruthless inflexibility she would never be free of her fear.

'I trust you,' she said as indifferently as she could.

'Why?' He looked almost disconcerted, and angry with it, as though he would like to cut through the cloak of indifference she wore and force out the woman who hid beneath.

'Because Geoffrey trusted you,' she said, cool irony hiding her thoughts. 'And Geoffrey was an excellent judge of character.'

'Before senile lust distorted his judgment,' he returned with cruel clarity. 'Do you wonder if I might be like him, Tiffany? Because if you are hoping for an affair with me, just remember one thing. I'm a vastly different proposition from my sick uncle, I promise you.'

Swift colour beat up beneath her skin then ebbed, leaving her white and drawn. 'Oh, I'm sure you are,' she retorted tonelessly. 'No, I'm not gunning for you, so you can relax. I dislike intensely macho men even when they're as nicely packaged as you.' Her chin lifted; it took will-power but she smiled serenely into the cold distaste of his face. 'I don't need your money. Geoffrey left me nicely provided for, and you can't offer me anything else I want.'

'No? Is that why you took an old man as your lover? Because you're frigid?'

He only just caught her wrist as it flew towards his

face. In a quick, painful movement he twisted it behind her back and hauled her close, holding her so that the tips of her breasts brushed the dark cloth of his suit.

More bruises, Tiffany thought bitterly, but this time she did not struggle. It was useless, and anyway she knew that physically he would not harm her. The threat he represented was not to her body but to her emotions and her will.

As the realisation of this truth hit her like the lash of a whip she clamped down on those emotions, intent on establishing control. For some reason his last taunt had succeeded where others had failed but she could not let him see it.

He knew, of course; he was too astute not to recognise her anger, however she hid it.

'You don't like being called frigid,' he observed with malice. 'I wonder why? Too close to the bone?'

'Get out,' she whispered raggedly. 'I don't care what you think of me, you can't despise me any more than I loathe you, you arrogant, stiff-necked, patronising b-beast!' Not even then could she break a lifetime's prohibitions and swear, but the effort to restrain herself was obvious. 'Who do you think you are, setting yourself up on a peak of morality when all the world knows that you—that you——'

'Go on,' he encouraged icily.

She threw her head back, staring at him with implacable dislike. 'You know what I mean. But of course it's different for a man. I'm a slut, but you're *experienced*! Sounds a lot better, doesn't it? Now get out of my house.'

'Gladly.' He spoke through clenched teeth as he dragged her hard against him. 'But first, let's just see, shall we, how close I came to the truth just then.'

Tiffany kicked out, twisting her head away to avoid the hard thrust of his mouth. For a moment she was aware that she wanted this, that every nerve in her body was exulting in the sensation of being pressed against him while his mouth forced a kiss on her. It was as if her body was possessed of instincts of its own, instincts which bypassed the thought processes of the brain. For a long breathless moment she stayed limp in his arms, not responding but not resisting, listening to what her body was trying to tell her.

Then he lifted his head and smiled down into her eyes. 'As I said,' he mocked silkily, 'frigid. A pity.'

'So you'll just have to look elsewhere for your next mistress,' she retorted, wiping her hand across her mouth and hating him, hating him.

'There was never any doubt about that,' he told her, stepping back. 'In spite of the fact that most authorities would have us believe that there is no such thing as a frigid woman, only inept men, I'll give it a miss. Not that it wouldn't be enjoyable to initiate you into the joys of sex. I find you quite appealing—or I would if I didn't feel unclean within ten feet of you.'

If he had still had his arms around her he would have felt her flinch at his vicious words. Indeed, she closed her eyes for a second so that he couldn't see her pain. But she lifted her chin to retort coolly, 'In that case, don't bother to come here again. If there's anything you want me to know a 'phone call will do.'

'Gladly. I'll see you at my office tomorrow morning at eleven. Can you get the time off work?'

'Oh yes,' she said with crisp composure. 'That's no problem.'

It rained that night, and continued the next day, not heavily but with a penetrating chill which was uncomfortable and depressing. As Tiffany tapped along the street towards the bus stop she took comfort from the glowing pinks and reds of the camellias in every garden. The dark, shiny foliage served as a magnificent backdrop for the great, waxy blooms. At their feet there were jonquils, their cheerful little yellow and white flowers scenting the damp air. Some gardens were gay with anemones, others chose the more subdued colours of violas and Dutch irises beneath the enormous pink canopy of magnolias. It was like spring yet there was another month of winter to go. A far cry from home, Tiffany thought, pierced by homesickness.

The bus was full, mostly of matronly ladies with shopping baskets and raincoats. One carried a bunch of violets and some sprigs of Japanese honeysuckle. Its sweet, spicy perfume floated around the bus like the breath of all the springs that had ever been. Tiffany's sadness lifted a little; she looked out at the gardens and houses, spotted a Rolls Royce and smiled at the antics of a small, white dog as it pranced down the street with its owner.

Queen Street, Auckland's main thoroughfare, was busy, the shop windows bright with next summer's fashions, a cheerful contrast to the universal rain-gear of the shoppers. Tiffany walked slowly along, peering into the windows of all the bookshops but too afraid of temptation to go in. Deciding to join the local library the next time she had time to spare she glanced at her watch and blinked. Somehow her window gazing had left her with only five minutes to get to Eliot's office. Fortunately it wasn't far away, but she arrived breathless and rather cross, only to be told by a very *soignée* receptionist that Mr Buchanan was busy and would she mind waiting? And taking a seat?

'No,' she said politely, and sat down, picking up a magazine. It was written for businessmen and was rather depressing about the economic situation. Worthwhile, no doubt, but it appeared to be written in a language which, although it bore a resemblance to English, was definitely not.

So she laid the magazine down and avoided the receptionist's far too interested gaze by staring remotely out of the window. The leather of the sofa was rich and opulent; after a few minutes it began to warm up. On the wall opposite was a painting, a very good one, Tiffany decided respectfully, of a tree. It was not completely realistic, there was not that photographic faithfulness to detail which she found boring, but as she looked at it she could feel the mysterious serenity of the bush.

The receptionist's lacquered fingernails flashed as she typed some impossible number of words per minute. But then, Eliot would have only the best. Probably the girl was in love with him. On the desk there was a bowl of daffodils. Behind the sofa an enormous indoor plant stretched out vigorous leaves. The carpet was plush, a dark subdued blue which, Tiffany decided, must be an absolute beast to keep clean, but clean it was, immaculately so. Naturally. Like the receptionist only the best would do.

Something made her mind click; scrabbling hastily in her bag she drew out a pen and her shopping list and made notes on something new for her range of table napkins. Engrossed in getting everything down before it fled from her mind, as it was likely to, she failed to hear a door opening. In fact, it wasn't until Eliot's shadow fell across her that she looked up, bemused.

'Oh, hallo,' she said nervously. He towered over her, only his eyes alive in the polished mask of his face.

'Good morning.'

Very formal. Not encouraged at all by the absorbed sideways glance of the receptionist, Tiffany stuffed the list and pen back into her bag as she scrambled to her feet, wishing that he didn't loom so far above her. Everything about him was intimidating, she thought wearily.

His office was big, with a desk which suited him, being of elegant Italian design, very modern, very efficient, very up-market. There was a bowl of glasshouse freesias in bright colours on the satiny wood, their sweet, evocative fragrance welcoming. Outside the rain drummed down past a small balcony ornamented by elaborate Victorian stonework.

'Does it meet with your approval?' he asked blandly.

Tiffany blinked again. 'Oh dear,' she sighed. 'Yes, it does. It's very—very *you*, as I'm sure you know. Who was your decorator?'

'My mother,' he said, and smiled narrowly at her astonishment.

'She has great talent,' she offered carefully.

He grinned at that. 'Oh, she has indeed, my mama.'
Then the amusement disappeared, leaving him cold and
ruthless. 'Right, let's get down to business, shall we?
Did you go through the list of jewellery last night?'

'No. Should I have?'

'Well, since the man is going to deliver it this
morning and you will be expected to sign a receipt, then
yes, I think you should have.'

'I see,' she shrugged. 'Well, I'll check the list against
the jewellery when it arrives. Shouldn't he be here now?'

'He should. Why don't you sit down while we wait
for him?'

The chair was comfortable, but Tiffany felt prickles
of unease through her skin. Across the shining expanse
of desk Eliot was very much the lawyer, very much in
control, and she didn't like it.

'Before he arrives there are a couple of things we
have to go through,' he said as he pushed a paper
towards her. 'Will you read that and tell me what you
understand by it?'

It was a somewhat complicated document relating to
the trust. Tiffany read it through with great care, asking
for several clarifications. After the third time the paper
had been pushed back and forth across the desk Eliot
got to his feet and came to stand behind her. Tiffany's
concentration immediately evaporated. It took all of
her will-power to force her mind from his closeness to
the legal document.

'You may find this a little unclear,' he said, bending
to point at a paragraph.

Tiffany looked at the lean brown finger and said, 'I
don't—oh, yes. It is, rather.'

The deep voice explained. Tiffany moved as far away
from him as the chair would allow. Tension began to
build, pulling at her nerves. It was as though she was
divided into two parts, the logical, emotionless brain
concentrating so hard on the paper and her body,
calling fiercely to his.

'. . . Geoffrey was very particular about that.' The deep voiced paused then said in exactly the same tone, 'Your hair smells like flowers.'

'Sh-shampoo,' she said in an indrawn breath. 'Or else it's the freesias.'

'No. I've noticed it before.' His voice came closer.

Tiffany held her breath. Her heart began to thud with quick, heavy strokes. The hands which had pointed out legal phrases moved, slid to curve her cheek and then to her chin, lifting her head to meet his. She looked up into eyes like blazing blue fires and said dazedly, 'I—no, Eliot . . .'

'Yes, Eliot,' he said, his mouth touching hers so softly that she shivered, her hands gripping the arms of the chair.

'Say "Yes, Eliot",' he whispered.

She could say nothing, but her lashes drooped and her mouth opened beneath his. A river of sensation was running golden through her veins yet their only points of contact were where their mouths met in the lightest, most tantalising kiss and his fingers beneath her chin.

'Say yes,' he said in between his teasing kisses.

Tiffany groaned and put out a hand. Whether to push him away or pull him closer she never knew. Her fingers slid over the warm dark material of his suit, moved beneath to where his heart thundered against the thin shirt. She felt an incredible urge to explore beneath his shirt, to find and touch the lean perfection of his body. Her fingertips tingled with expectation and need, all the more acute for being totally new to her. Slowly she closed her eyes, visualising him as he would be ready for love. Colour brushed her cheeks; she was tormented by desire, her body so sensitised to his that she could almost feel the brush of his skin against her, the weight . . .

Her head jerked back as she realised just where his teasing caresses and her too vivid imagination were taking her.

'No,' she gasped, using her hand to push at him.

'Don't be silly.' He too was breathing heavily, his expression set as he used her hand to pull her out of the chair and into his arms. He looked—out of control, she thought with a tremor of fear. But Eliot didn't ever lose control. And she wished that she knew more about men because perhaps then she would understand his actions.

Fear was swept away as he groaned and bent his head to capture her mouth in a kiss so seducingly sweet that she could not resist him.

'Relax,' he muttered, his breath warm in her mouth. 'I swear I'm not going to hurt you. I swear—oh God, you torment me . . .'

She frowned then lifted the hands which had been crushed between them and shaped his face. Beneath them his skin was fever-hot, its fine texture damp. Tiffany was afraid yet the desire in her own body drove her to respond to him with all of the fervour of a naturally ardent temperament.

Before, when he kissed her, he had been the one in control; it had been his restraint which had stopped the embrace. Now that guarded self-possession was gone. Something had slipped the leash and she was shattered by its intensity, afraid because she knew that there was no way she could get through to him. He seemed almost oblivious to her, lost in a world of feverish desire as his mouth roamed her face, tasting the soft skin with sensuous enjoyment.

And she responded with her own magic, finding the warm strength of his throat with open-mouthed kisses, her tongue touching the salty skin. Passion began to claw at her so that she pressed herself against him, lost to everything but the sensations he was calling to life in every cell in her body.

CHAPTER FOUR

THE telephone shrilled its intrusive summons. For a moment they both stood frozen as though they had been caught robbing a safe.

Eliot let her go, so abruptly that she stumbled and almost fell into the chair. The blind hunger in his eyes faded. He stared down at her and she cringed as she saw unsparing scorn replace it.

His lips moved; she did not know what word he said below his breath, but it hurt her like a knife wound across tender skin.

He reached out a still-shaking hand and barked, 'Yes.'

After a moment he said, 'I'll be ready in a moment,' and put it down. 'That's the jeweller,' he told her remotely.

'I—I see.' Nervously she ran a hand through her hair; it had been ruffled by the hand which had held her head still. She could still feel the strength of the fingers across her scalp.

Now she knew why so many women had, in her stepfather's idiom, 'got into trouble'. The ache she was feeling now had to be frustration and it hurt, it made her want to scream. Her breasts felt swollen and as tender as her mouth. There was nothing she wanted more that to follow the road he had beguiled her down to its destination.

She could not, of course. If he loved her—even if he liked her—then it would have been hard to resist him. But he felt nothing but contempt for her and she could not bear to see again the change in his expression when he realised who he had been making love to.

It was this thought which fired her blood with anger and brought her head up. She had not begun it—she had never been the one to start. Eliot had, with his tormenting mouth and hands. What right had he to kiss her so—so *sweetly* one moment and then the next look at her as if she was something particularly nasty from under a stone!

'Are you ready?' he asked with peremptory abruptness.

'Yes.'

He looked at her as though he could hardly bear to. 'You had better put some lipstick on.'

'And you had better wipe some off,' she retorted.

With a gesture of disgust he pulled out an immaculate handkerchief and wiped the betraying stain from his lips before, remote and isolated behind his desk, her rang the receptionist.

The man from the jeweller's was pleasant, young enough to appreciate Tiffany's smile and figure before his glance collided with the bleak frost that was Eliot's. This brought about an immediate change in his manner. He became respectful, almost deferential as they all three went over the list. Then Tiffany signed a receipt at the bottom, and the receptionist appeared like a genie to usher the jeweller out, leaving behind her a strange, tense silence.

Not looking at him, Tiffany said awkwardly, 'Well, thank you. I'll go now.'

'I'll run you home.'

'No,' she said, angered by his brusqueness, 'I'll be fine.'

'I'll run you home just the same. Individually those pieces are not worth much, but collectively they represent quite an amount.'

He spoke with inflection, his expression aloof and immensely self-contained.

'Then I'll get a taxi,' Tiffany said obstinately.

'Just do as you're told, will you.' And when she remained seated in the chair he swung around the desk and deliberately wound his fingers in the curls at the nape of her neck so that her head was jerked back. 'Or

I'll have to force you to,' he said softly through lips which hardly moved. 'And you wouldn't like that. Or perhaps you would—too much.'

The unconcealed menace made her swallow nervously. His glance dropped to the pale, bared line of her throat, resting there with all the impact of a blow.

'All right,' she said huskily, thinking, of all things, that he could no longer call her frigid now.

He said nothing on the way home, concentrating with bleak efficiency on his driving.

But at the doorway, after he had greeted an ecstatic Jess, he said coldly. 'I doubt if I'll be seeing you again for a while. I have to go overseas.'

'Oh.'

He looked down at her, the mask firmly in place, yet unable to hide a hunger which made her take a swift step backwards.

'Aren't you going to kiss me goodbye?' he said, each word a separate sneer.

Tiffany shook her head, unable to repress the shudder his words caused.

'No? Perhaps you're wise.' He had been carrying the case which held the jewellery. Now he jerked it forward. 'Here you are—take your loot.'

'Just put it down,' she returned without expression.

So he did, and turned to go. Then he swung back, but whatever he had been going to say was lost as he swore, one short, sharp expletive, and caught her in his arms, bending her back so that he loomed over her, his mouth hard and seeking on her throat. His hand slid up between the soft material of her shirt and her slip and closed gently over her breast, sending an arrow of sensation through her which headed for the pit of her stomach.

'No!' she gasped, but his mouth covered hers, invaded it with a demand for total surrender and, between the hot seduction of the kiss and the incredible needles of desire his clever, experienced fingers wrung from her too-responsive flesh, she was lost.

Tremors shook her as his fingers explored the gentle contours of her breast, moving inexorably to the sensitive nub at the centre. When they reached it she groaned, her eyes heavy and slumberous, their darkness banished by glowing gold lights.

Then it was over. She felt cold and aching as he said harshly, 'Don't look at me like that! Call it a reward—for me.'

'What—what for?'

She wasn't interested, barely knew what she was saying, but somehow she had to clear her mind of the unfulfilled yearning which was shaking her.

'For using my influence on your behalf.' He flung her a black, totally contemptuous glance then walked away. 'I must be mad,' he said savagely as he opened the door.

It took time for the turmoil his lovemaking had produced to subside. That night when Tiffany prepared for bed she still felt heavy-headed, her bones aching.

The next morning she had a raging headache and the kind of temperature which makes feverish seem an understatement. Her throat was sore and her whole body felt wrenched and racked. It took all of her effort to get downstairs to feed Jess. She had to sit for ten minutes before she could tackle the stairs again.

What she had assumed to be frustration was a virus, a particularly vigorous one. But if that day was bad the next was worse. She developed a hard cough which hurt her lungs, and whenever she moved her head it felt as though it was going to snap off at the neck. Limp and exhausted, she couldn't find the energy to prepare meals. Possibly this accounted for some of her exhaustion. The rest of it was probably caused by the frequency with which she sneezed and coughed.

She swallowed down more aspirin and drank as much water as she could, and spent all of that day dozing off, waking only to cough or sneeze. Late in the afternoon the doorbell woke her up again. She hoped that it was Mrs Crowe, back from Gisborne. Slowly she pulled on her dressing-gown and slippers before making her way with weary effort down the stairs.

It was not her neighbour. It was Eliot. He took one look at her and went white beneath his tan.

'It's just a bug,' she whispered, so glad to see him that she could have drooped against him and wept. 'I thought you were away.'

'I came back early. This is not *just* anything.' He picked her up and carried her back up the stairs. 'How long have you been like this?'

'Two days, I think,' she said, blissfully leaning her head against the hard wall of his chest.

'Have you been to the doctor?'

She chuckled but it turned into a cough and she was back in her tumbled bed before the paroxysm ended. It left her sore and breathless but she said, 'I don't think I'd get there, do you?'

He muttered something beneath his breath then picked her up again and set her on the floor. The wall was cool to her cheek. She leaned against it dreamily, admiring his efficiency as he stripped and remade the bed. Before he started he had hung his coat over the door handle; she liked the play of his muscles beneath the pale material of his shirt. Now that he was here she was only too willing to give up fighting the virus. He would take care of her.

'You need a bath,' he said when he had finished. 'No, a shower would be better. Do you think you can get yourself in and out?'

She nodded. But he said, 'I'll wait outside the door. If you need any help, yell out, OK?'

Nodding again she tried to get to her feet but her muscles refused to obey and she looked mutely at him.

'Have you had any food at all?' he asked harshly, helping her up and holding her a moment against him.

She shook her head. It hurt, so she said, 'No, but I haven't felt like any, truly, Eliot.'

'You're too young to be let out,' he said grimly, but he was very gentle as he guided her across to the bathroom. 'Where do you keep your nightdresses?'

It took her a moment to remember but she did it, and even managed to walk into the shower without his supporting arm. The water was warm and soothing on her tired body. She was too slow to avoid wetting her hair, and anyway, it seemed a good idea to wash it. Even that exhausted her, however. She was leaning against the wall of the shower stall, eyes closed, when he opened the door and turned the rose off.

'That's long enough,' he said.

Tiffany knew that she should be extremely wary of such intimacy, and she also knew that she was not. She smiled trustingly at him as he wrapped a bath towel around her and another round her wet curls.

'I don't know that you should have washed your hair,' he said, steering her across to the bed, 'but as it makes you look about twelve it's probably a good thing.'

She sighed and he sat her down and towel-dried her hair before saying briskly, 'Right, can you get into your nightdress?'

'Yes,' she said like an obedient child.

'I'll go down and do some ringing up.'

It took her while but she managed to pull on the one he got out for her, a childish thing of brushed cotton, buttoned up to the neck with long sleeves. When he came back she was coughing again, wiping the tears from her eyes with crumpled handkerchief.

'Have you got a hair dryer?' he asked.

'No.'

His hand touched a curl near her face. 'It's almost dry. All right, into bed with you. Does that feel better?'

It felt like heaven. The sheets were cool and clean against her clean body and although she was still swimming in the head she stayed upright, smiling mistily at him.

'Thank you,' she said. 'I'll be fine now.'

Unfortunately her wretched cough gave the lie to this. While it lasted she had to hunch over, her arms folded over her chest, taking shallow, painful breaths.

When she felt his arm round her shoulders she turned gratefully to him, drawing on his strength. His hand moved gently over her back, stroking, almost rubbing. It did seem to ease the pain but she protested.

'You mustn't. I'll give you the bug.'

'I'm never ill,' he said, his voice reverberating through the walls of his chest. 'Lie down and I'll get you something to drink.'

He was gone for a little while and when he reappeared he was bearing a tray, while Jess, triumphant and smug, trotted at his heels.

'Eat,' he said softly. 'My scrambled eggs are famous and I'll be angry if you turn them down.'

For two days she had not felt in the least hungry, but when he set the tray down in front of her she was overcome by hunger pangs.

'It looks delicious,' she said. 'Where did you get the tray?'

'Mrs Crowe. She's just arrived home.'

It was delicious, the smooth curds sliding easily past her sore throat. She ate slowly but with great enjoyment, finishing just as the doorbell rang again.

'That will be the doctor,' Eliot informed her as he removed the tray.

'Oh.'

The doctor was about Eliot's age, a small, thin, sandy man who smiled at her with professional kindness and firmly banished Eliot and Jess. After ten minutes of tapping and listening and thermometer reading and pulse-checking he invited them both back in again and said severely, 'A bad case of bronchitis and that sneezing is sinusitis. Not helped by semi-starvation.'

Tiffany could feel guilt mark her face but the doctor went on, 'I'll give you a prescription, an antibiotic as well as tablets and a syrup for the cough, and you will stay in bed for at least another two days, and inside, if you have any sense, until the end of the week. And eat!'

Brushing aside her thanks he left. She could hear him talking to Eliot below for some minutes, then came the slam of the door and Eliot's footsteps on the stairs again.

'I'll go and get the prescription,' he said. 'I've found a key in your bag so I'll let myself in.'

She nodded but as he turned to go said, 'Eliot?' He looked back over his shoulder and she whispered, 'Thank you.'

He said nothing but he gave her a long look, the meaning of which she was still trying to decide when sleep overtook her.

The tablets had a peculiar effect on her, making her head even more muzzy than it was before, but she retained enough sense to protest at some stage of the evening, 'You can't stay here, Eliot. You must go home.'

'And spend all the night worrying about you?' he asked roughly.

'But your mother—and there's no place for you to sleep.'

'I've rung my mother. As for sleeping—there's a sofa.'

Bemusedly she shook her head, hot tears making her feel exhausted. 'You're so kind,' she whispered.

'Kind?' The word was a harsh expletive as though she had insulted him. 'No, I'm not being kind, my dear.'

She stared at him, her forehead wrinkled as she tried to see beyond the dark mask of his expression. The blue eyes were filled with leaping little lights which fascinated her. She stretched out a hand, thin and trembling, and took his warm, strong one.

'Yes you are,' she said and pulled it down so that she could hold it between her cheek and the pillow.

She slept like that, waking only once during the night with a throat like sandpaper. Eliot's voice was wonderfully soothing, his hands gentle as he propped her up and gave her one of the painkillers the doctor had prescribed.

She sighed and said, 'Don't go,' and slept again, to wake in the morning with the fever broken and her head resting confidingly on his shoulder, his arm holding her against the lean length of his body.

Her throat hurt, her nose was blocked and when she breathed a faint wheeze warned her that her lungs were still fighting infection, but she had never felt so happy in her life. A bubble of joy, pure and ethereal, began somewhere in her heart, inflating to colour her whole life with its rainbow hues. The moment was supremely precious; she lay quietly, eyes closed, feeling the warmth of his body against her. His skin was very smooth, but even in the relaxation of sleep the body beneath it was hard with muscles. Probably formed by the same activity which gave him that year-round tan. She could hear his heart, a solid, even thunder, totally reliable in its regularity. The arm across her was curved so that his hand rested on her hip; she thought that even through the brushed material of her nightdress she could feel each separate fingertip and wondered fancifully if she was going to be marked for life by five incredibly sensitive spots there. He was warm and solid and she wondered what it would be like to have him move his warm, exciting mouth over her throat and further down . . . to slide his hand the length of her body . . .

Stupid, *stupid* to let herself make such speculations! Immediately her body was racked with an agony of desire which terrified her. She thought she heard a change in the deep, regular breathing and stiffened. He muttered something and turned, resting his chin on her curls, enclosing her in the protective warmth of his arms. Safe, sheltered from the world, she smiled and drifted back off to sleep.

When she woke again she was alone in the bed. For several moments she lay quietly, wondering why she should feel so abandoned, until memory returned and she turned her head. There was no trace of him. Even the pillow had been smoothed.

Had it been just a dream? How could she keep her distance when her subconscious did this to her? Whipping over in the bed she turned her head into the pillow and groaned. But no, it had been no dream. She remembered her dreams. They had been erotic fantasies which made her scarlet to even think of them, but the overwhelming memory of waking in his arms had been simple security.

And it would be as dangerous to become addicted to that as it would be to fall victim to his overpowering sensual promise, thought Tiffany bitterly.

When he came up the stairs she had washed her face and cleaned her teeth, taken the various tablets and potions prescribed for her, and was sitting on the side of the bed combing her hair. It was in a complete tangle, and she winced as the comb snarled. Her scalp felt tender and sore, like the rest of her skin.

'Here, let me do that,' he said, setting the tray down on the chest of drawers, which was the only other piece of furniture in the room.

'No, I'm quite—I can do it.' She couldn't prevent the colour which flooded her skin. Her eyes slid sideways and her lashes flickered. It was totally impossible that they should have shared the same bed, yet the remembrance of what it had been like was seared into her brain—and her body.

He looked impatient and took her hairbrush from the chest. 'This will be easier,' he decided.

The comb stilled in her hand. Her sudden shyness had forced her to turn away from him.

She felt the side of the bed go down as he sat behind her. Slowly she took her hand from her hair and sat with it in her lap, her knuckles whitening as they clenched the comb.

His touch was very deft and sure. 'Incredible,' he remarked after a moment. 'Is it a perm or natural?'

'It's natural.' Her voice shook so she took a breath and steadied it. 'I was born with curls.'

'Mm.' The brush moved carefully, coaxing the fine, thick tresses into order. With a note of mockery in his voice he said, 'I woke this morning with a confused idea of having grown a very itchy beard during the night. It was quite a relief to find that it was only your mop tickling my chin.'

'Oh,' she said in a very small voice.

He chuckled and got to his feet. 'You were right, the sofa was unbearable, so I came up and made myself at home. You didn't seem to mind.'

She could not prevent herself from turning to see what he meant. He was looking at her with the sardonic amusement she hated, lashes hiding his eyes and that cruel, beautiful mouth half-smiling.

'I told you you shouldn't have stayed,' she said with a defiant glare.

'Nonsense. I enjoyed sleeping in your bed,' he said coolly and deliberately. 'Even if you did cough a lot. One of these nights there'll be no coughing and I'll take what you were offering me when you moved so confidingly into my arms.'

'I was asleep,' she cried, angered by the sneering words.

'Yes, you were, and I've no doubt that you'd have welcomed anyone just as sweetly and sensuously. Get under the blankets.'

She shook her head, unnerved by his attack, yet in spite of it prey to a kind of tormenting sensuality at his promise for the future.

'No, don't cry,' he said now, 'you'll spoil your appetite. Are you going to get in or will I put you?'

The tears ran down her cheeks and she sniffed and wiped them away with the fingers of one hand while her other searched the pocket of her dressing-gown for a handkerchief. Eliot gave an exclamation of irritation and disappeared downstairs. When he came back bearing the chair she used for sewing she was back in bed, blowing her nose.

'Why on earth don't you get some furniture?' he asked, dumping the chair down beside her. 'I sent you an advance.'

'I have what is necessary,' she said thickly.

'As far as I'm concerned a bedside table is a

necessity.' He brought the tray across and deposited it on her lap, adding as she straightened up, 'I have to go now—I have an early appointment, but I'll give Mrs Crowe the key and she can come in and see you.'

She lifted a dismayed face. 'But I don't want—or need—her,' she protested, meeting his inflexible regard with one just as steady.

'She's offered to make you lunch,' he went on as though she hadn't spoken. 'I'll be back round about six tonight. Remember what the doctor said. *No* getting up.'

'I'll get up when I want.' She was scarlet with anger, the golden highlights in her eyes sparkling and snapping in their depths. 'You needn't think that I'm going to be bullied just because I've been a little sick. I'm not——'

He put a finger across her mouth and she stopped in mid-word because the touch of his finger called forth such a response that it was like a clamour in her blood.

'You'll do just as you're told,' he said, clearly bored. 'Or I'll hire a nurse to sit with you.'

The finger was removed. Her eyes darkened into mutiny and the soft gentleness of her mouth hardened into a straight line but she said nothing.

'Be a good girl,' he said, and astounded her by bending and kissing her forehead like a favourite uncle. 'You don't want me to worry about you, do you?'

As a parting shot it was excellent. While she ate the half-grapefruit and toast he had prepared Tiffany decided that it was a taunt, but she knew that she lied to herself. For all his arrogance and high-handedness Eliot really did care about people. It was a miracle to hear his voice soften when he mentioned his mother and he had loved Geoffrey enough to give up a lot of his time to entertaining him. He liked Jess; he was a cynic when it did not affect his attitude towards the self-seeking, rather foolish people he considered most of humanity to be.

The coffee was delicious, refreshing her just by its fragrance. As she drank it she remembered one evening when Geoffrey was alive and the television news had recounted a double murder, deliberately planned. She had been horrified and said so, wondering what sort of person could do such a dreadful thing.

And Eliot had shrugged and drawled, 'Ordinary people, Tiffany.'

'Ordinary people don't murder,' she objected, enjoying the occasion to cross swords with him.

'Most ordinary people have the seeds of murder in them. If you don't believe that it's only because you've never been where murder has seemed the only logical action.'

He had laughed at her refusal to accept that and in his smooth legal voice said, 'Right, let's use our imagination. I don't suppose you're particularly maternal so we'll try a different tack. There must be someone you love, desperately, fervently, someone who depends on you?'

His crack about her lack of maternal emotions hurt and she shook her head even as an image of her younger brother Peter sprang to her mind.

'Well,' Eliot resumed patiently, 'can you imagine your own child, clinging desperately to you as you and she are threatened by a man with a knife. You know that he is quite capable of using it—he is, shall we say, your estranged husband. The child is not his and he knows it and has told you that he plans to kill you both.'

The deep voice paused on a note of enquiry. Beneath the coolness there was a different note. Tiffany realised with a flat anger that he had chosen the story deliberately, using it as yet another way to ram home his contempt for her.

'You know,' he went on mercilessly, 'that his jealousy and his torment are such that he is capable of doing that. In the drawer close by your right hand is a loaded gun; your child is crying and clinging to your legs. And you see the knife and the implacable purpose in your husband's eyes as he begins to move towards you. What do you do?'

Fine hairs all down her spine stood erect. More to silence him than anything else she capitulated. 'Shoot him, of course.' Her voice sounded odd, uneven. She had to steady it before adding, 'But not to kill, if I could possibly help it. However, you've proved your point.'

He smiled, watching her with half-closed eyes. 'No, you proved it,' he drawled. 'Any action can be excused—is always excused. Few suffer remorse and anguish because it is far easier to justify their actions. How else do you think anyone can live with themselves? A thief, a rapist, a murderer can usually tell us exactly why it was necessary to do what they have done.'

She had argued against such a cynical observation. The subsequent conversation had been exciting and stimulating and when he used anecdotes from his profession to back up his assertions, she had been fascinated.

After he had gone Geoffrey had smiled and said, 'He's a tale-teller, is Eliot. Do you believe that we reveal ourselves every time we open our mouths?'

'I suppose we do.'

'Then I wonder,' her father said, still smiling, 'just exactly what was the meaning of that little scenario he came up with to prove that you'd kill, given the right situation.'

'It means he doesn't like me,' she said tartly, humiliated again.

'Do you think so?' And Geoffrey had looked as though he was very pleased with life. 'I think it meant that he sees you as a very dangerous woman. For him, anyway.'

Now, with the cup empty of the coffee he had made for her she thought that perhaps Geoffrey had been more perceptive than she. She had not realised then the unwilling attraction which had sprung full-blown into life at their first meeting. It had not occurred to her that attraction could be masked by dislike or, in Eliot's case, contempt. Of course he had recognised it.

Geoffrey had, too. She could see now why her father had encouraged Eliot to visit him in spite of her occasional protests. In his own quiet way he was a matchmaker, not realising that Eliot had made up his mind right from the start that she was unprincipled and greed, with the morals of a slut

What if she should tell him just who she was? If he demanded it she had Geoffrey's letter as proof, and she would like to watch his face as he realised how wrong he had been. And as he had the kind of integrity which has sharp edges on it there would be no danger of Marie's secret leaking out.

But Marie had asked that no one be told. Eliot might feel that his loyalty to his relations, Diane March and Colin Upcott, made it necessary to tell them. And Geoffrey had counselled caution and delay.

She told herself that that was the reason why she kept her secret. Not to herself, not even in the solitude of her bedroom, would she admit that she was too afraid to tell him. For what if she did, and he still looked at her with the same contempt and dislike? A hope so barely recognised that it was unformed would be slain stillborn. And there would be nothing left for her but to go away.

That afternoon she was lying sleepily in bed when Mrs Crowe let herself in with the key Eliot had given her.

'It's just me, Tiffany,' she called.

Earlier in the day Tiffany had apologised to her for Eliot's high-handedness but the old woman laughed.

'Nonsense, don't be silly. I would be a hopeless sort of neighbour if I just ignored you,' she said cheerfully, adding with a twinkle, 'as for your Mr Buchanan, I like a bit of arrogance in a man. I know it's not fashionable to admit it but a good strong man is just what every woman needs. And don't tell me that you didn't welcome him taking over last night.'

And Tiffany had to admit that she had.

Now Mrs Crowe appeared with tea. She sat on the

chair and sipped tea and gossiped quietly about the other inhabitants of the row. Half-way through a mildly scandalous little tale the doorbell rang.

'Ah yes,' Mrs Crowe said. 'Mr Buchanan warned me to expect this. Would you like to put your dressing-gown on and wait in the bathroom?'

'But who——?'

'It's a surprise,' Mrs Crowe told her archly.

Perched on the side of the bath Tiffany decided that she must be sicker than she had thought. The house was well built but she could hear masculine voices from her bedroom. They appeared to be moving about for some time. Then there were just Mrs Crowe's footsteps, barely discernible, pattering to and fro. And instead of rushing out to see what was going on Tiffany sat quietly like an obedient child. It must be the tablets. They certainly made her feel dopey; clearly they made her act that way, too.

When at last she was lethargically summoning up the strength to get up and see what was going on Mrs Crowe flung the door open, her face alive and excited.

'Have a look,' she invited.

At first Tiffany couldn't believe her eyes. The furniture she had bought was gone. In its place was a sleek, streamlined bed—double, she noted with increasing outrage, and flanked by bedside tables—and a dressing-table surrounded by an enormous mirror. It was all beautiful, and clearly extremely expensive.

'Oh,' she said weakly.

'I shouldn't have kept you up so long,' Mrs Crowe said with remorse as she urged her across and into the bed, already made up with percale sheets and an enormous, feather-light duvet covered in gold and green. 'But I did so want it to be a complete surprise. Now, lie back and I'll make you another cup of tea.'

Because there was nothing else she could do Tiffany did that, even managed to laugh at Jess's antics when she sniffed her way around the unfamiliar furniture. But, weak as she was, the anger which had seared through her as she realised what Eliot had done didn't decrease. In fact it built up so that by the time he had said he was coming back she was sitting upright in the enormous hateful bed, her eyes fever-bright, a hard flush of colour along her cheekbones.

The first intimation of his arrival was Jess's excited barking. Then there were the sounds of voices from below as he and Mrs Crowe conferred, her eyes fixed with painful intensity on the door.

Her fury when he didn't immediately come up appalled her. But it was nothing compared to the emotions which swept her when his voice came up the stairs.

'I'll take Jess out now, Tiffany.'

'*Oh!*' she spat through gritted teeth. 'Oh—you—you *swine!*'

But he was gone.

Half an hour later, when he arrived back, she had showered and changed her nightgown, taken her tablets and the vile cough mixture and was ready, mentally and physically, for the fight.

He appeared at the door, tall and dark and dominating, his expression bored.

Tiffany opened her mouth for the attack. Before she had a chance to speak he held up a hand.

'I am not going to fight with you,' he said coolly. 'Any other time, certainly, but not tonight. You're not well enough to give it your usual effort, and I'll take nothing but the best from you.'

'You'll get *nothing* from me,' she declared fiercely.

'Not tonight, not even the rough side of your tongue,' he agreed. 'If you want, you can repay me when the will is probated. Until then, not a single word about it.'

Balked of the confrontation she had geared herself for all afternoon she glowered at him in impotent rage. 'Why a double bed?' she demanded. 'If you think——'

His brows lifted. 'I didn't like any of the single ones,' he told her as though it was the obvious reason. 'Besides, a double bed is much more comfortable. I sleep in one.'

'No doubt. But I sleep alone!'

He laughed at that scathing rejoinder and came over and sat down on the side of the offending bed, preventing her instinctive withdrawal by grabbing her wrists.

'Not last night you didn't,' he jeered, and watched the blush that overlaid her anger and annoyance.

Relenting suddenly he released her and got up. 'Calm down, spitfire, and relax. I am not going to fight with you tonight and that's final. Your nose is red, your eyes are puffy, you obviously still have a slight temperature and you are reining in a cough with the utmost difficulty. I'm not a sadist!'

'You could have fooled me,' she muttered, self-conscious at his appraisal of her appearance. Not that he had been taunting her; in fact, he sounded almost affectionate.

That night he slept on the sofa and the night after that he went home, because the doctor's pills and potions had taken effect and she was well on the way to recovery.

Tiffany lay in the bed he had so high-handedly bought and listened to the night sounds. Since the day the bed had arrived he had been coolly polite, like a courteous but infinitely remote host. Yet even when he was at his most distant, memories of the embraces they had exchanged were deep in the heavy-lidded eyes. Tension, a kind of crackling energy which frightened yet excited her, was always between them. Like a barrier, she thought fuzzily, then, as she slipped into sleep, no, like ropes pulling them together, bonds neither of them wanted but which they were unable to escape.

CHAPTER FIVE

HE came back on Friday evening with a document for her to sign. One glance told her that the truce engendered by her illness was over. Not that his expression gave anything away, but behind the austere mask she felt anger and that terrible, debilitating scorn.

And when she had read the document through he said caustically, 'Are you sure that you wouldn't prefer to have your own lawyer check it? I might be cheating you, for all you know.'

'I doubt it,' she retorted, her diction crisp and angry, 'Geoffrey trusted you.'

He said nothing but something ugly gleamed behind the thick lashes as he looked down at her.

After a moment the wide shoulders moved in a slight shrug. 'So sign it.'

She did and handed it back to him. He was casually dressed in trousers which revealed powerfully muscled thighs and the long length of legs. In spite of the rain which spattered the windows he wore only a shirt, and that short-sleeved. His arms were as tanned as his face and neck. Tiffany found herself wondering again what sport it was that gave him that colour all year round.

Something caught in her throat; she swallowed, not realising that his eyes caught the betraying play of the small muscles beneath the clear pale olive of her skin.

It seemed to grow hot. Breathlessly she asked, 'Would you like a cup of coffee?'

'No, thank you.'

'Then—thank you.'

'For what?' His voice was rough, very slightly slurred as though like her he was having some difficulty in articulating the words.

Tiffany drew a short, sharp breath, suddenly afraid

to look at him. With her eyes fixed firmly on the spot where a pulse beat at the skin in the hollow of his throat she said quickly, 'For being so kind when I was ill.'

'Kind?' He made an obscenity of the word, following it with a humourless laugh. 'That wasn't kindness, Tiffany. Don't pretend to be naïve. A woman who sells herself to a senile old man has no right to adopt the attitudes of innocence.'

He was spoiling for a fight. There was a kind of leashed savagery in him which frightened her. Opening her mouth to repay contempt for contempt her eyes scanned his face. She saw the strange waiting look in his eyes and knew with a thrill of fear that she could not.

It hurt, but she forced a conciliatory note into her voice to mask the fear and anger. 'You were kind,' she said quietly as she turned towards the door, making it clear that she expected him to go.

'Then perhaps I deserve some recompense for my kindness.'

It hadn't worked. His sneering, silky voice made it plain that her attempt to appease whatever demon was tearing at him now had failed. Before she had time to try again he had dropped the document on to the table and caught her, his arms enveloping her in a crushing grip. Gasping with pain she lifted her head indignantly and his mouth swooped.

A long time later, when the blood was drumming in her ears and throat, he lifted his cruel, probing mouth and stared down into her face. She could feel tremors shaking the strong, elegant body and they bewildered her. Completely unconscious of what she did, she slid her arms around his shoulders, holding him firmly. A moment ago she had been furious, his black enchantment of her senses only adding to her rage. Now a strange and awkward tenderness filled her. She didn't know what to do.

'Oh, God,' he muttered, his face drawn. He looked exhausted, almost haunted; as she watched his eyes

closed and he began to kiss her, tiny little kisses across
the high line of her cheeks, tracing out the contours of
her face with his mouth.

'You're driving me crazy.' The words were barely
understandable, his voice was so thick.

Tiffany wanted only to ease the weary heaviness she
saw in him. Her arms tightened and she rubbed her
cheek against him, almost flinching at the heat of his
skin.

'Don't,' she whispered, not really aware of what she
was saying. 'Eliot, don't.'

'I must.'

His mouth found hers again, but this time there was no
cruelty in the deep kiss. It joined them in an embrace from
which neither desired to escape. His mouth was ravenous,
tasting her, shattering her, so that she responded with the
same feverish intensity, her small hands fastening on to
his shoulders, as mindlessly, endlessly, she experienced
only that hot tide of sensation which seemed to be centred
in the core of her body. It radiated through her, making
her groan with unselfconscious pleasure as his hands
began their wanton exploration of her body. Her skin
tingled then throbbed; she made no effort to stop him
when he pulled her T-shirt free of her skirt and unclipped
her bra.

His eyes roamed the soft contours of her breasts with
glazed adoration. In a hoarse, heavy voice he said, 'You
are so beautiful . . .' and before she could recover from
this assault on her emotions he pulled the shirt and bra
over her head.

For a moment cold reason stared at her. She stiffened
but his head bent, his mouth captured the hardened nub
of one breast and such ravishing sensations pierced her
body that she was lost.

Her whole body jerked in an agony of exquisite
pleasure; the muffled sound from her lips died as his
mouth moved, tracing a wildfire path to where the
other breast throbbed. Tiffany's head was flung back,
her eyes barely open, her skin flushed hectically.

Dazedly she thought, I shall die, I shall die, and still his mouth tormented her with an ecstasy of forbidden sensations.

She was not even aware that he had picked her up, but her body mourned the cessation of sensation and as he carried her up the stairs she opened her eyes—to the sudden realisation of what was going to happen up there, on the bed he had bought probably for just this purpose.

If she hadn't been so overwhelmed by her first experience of passion she might have managed things better. One glance at the set mask of his face should have warned her that she could not hope to escape unless she was very careful. Lust, she thought, appalled; I have seen lust personified, and her eyes fell to her half-naked body, cold now and aching with a pain she could not classify.

But because she was still more than half under the influence of his lovemaking, her brain cloudy and drugged, she said the first thing that came into her head.

'No!'

They had reached the top of the stairs and Eliot was half-way to the bedroom door. He appeared not to have heard her.

'No,' she said again, her voice high and frightened. 'I can't, Eliot. Please . . .'

She saw the change in his expression as his brain reacted to her words. The passion faded but did not disappear and anger, a bleak, implacable anger took its place.

Terrified and shamed though she was, she welcomed it. It was something she could deal with.

'I'm sorry,' she said as he stopped. Her tongue slid along suddenly dry lips; she winced as his eyes followed the small movement.

'So am I,' he said and continued on to the bed, dropping her on to it with a suddenness which temporarily robbed her of initiative.

She gaped, then panicked as she saw him wrench his shirt over his head. When his hands reached the buckle of his belt she made a harsh sobbing moan and tried to scramble from the bed. He held her still by the simple expedient of coming down to lie half on top of her while his head bent and he kissed her, using all of his strength to force her head back into the pillows. His hands stroked the satin skin from her waist to where her breasts were flattened beneath the broad hard plane of his chest.

She felt him, was crushed by his weight, unbearably stimulated by his scent and the hard evidence of his arousal, but she knew that she could not allow him to take her. By now intelligence had seeped in to replace the drugging desire which had clouded her brain; she realised her mistake of a moment ago and was not going to repeat it.

So when the brutal kiss was over she raised her hands and touched his face as it greedily sought her throat. 'I'm sorry,' she whispered, trying to force some sense into his head. 'But I can't do this, Eliot. Please, don't rape me.'

But the ugly word did not deter him. He lifted his head and smiled down at her. Tiffany flinched at the set savagery she saw in his expression, the merciless determination.

'It won't be rape,' he said, almost calmly. 'By the time I've finished with you, you little slut, you'll be begging on your knees for it.'

Appalled, she gazed up at him, her mouth trembling. When at last she could speak he was pressing slow, wide-lipped kisses on to the smooth contours of her shoulders, his hand stroking the skin at her waist with tormenting gentleness.

Shivering, because she wanted that hand, that mouth, on her more than anything else in the world, she tried to bring him back to sanity.

'Not like this,' she groaned. 'Not in anger.'

And he laughed, his breath scorching across her skin. 'It would have to be in anger,' he said ruthlessly, letting her hear his contempt. 'However seductive you are, you rouse mainly anger in me. But I'll enjoy you—and you will enjoy me, I promise you.'

He spoke like a man dedicating himself to vengeance. Tiffany's body jerked in negation; he laughed again and held her still while she struggled desperately until at last her strength evaporated and she lay half beneath him, a prisoner in his arms, and stared mutely up at him, her eyes glossed with tears.

Then he used his strength to pull her clothes from her, until her body lay, fair and flinching, for the harsh appraisal of his leaping, predatory gaze. Tiffany turned her head along the pillow, seeing herself as he saw her, a sacrifice laid out for his pleasure.

She willed herself to remain rigid and unresponsive to his caresses but her untutored body was no match for the experienced seduction he brought to his task, and long before he finally pressed his attack home she was on fire for him, logic and intelligence eclipsed by the tumult of the senses his clever, knowledgeable seduction brought to her downfall.

She even welcomed that first, painful thrust, watching with dilated, feverish eyes as comprehension blazed in his face. But he was so far beyond control that he could do nothing but obey the driving dictates of his passion, losing himself in the sweet femininity that he had taken for his own. Tiffany sighed, a little choked sound in that world of deep, harsh breathing and began to move with him, her hands fastening on to the sweat-slicked shoulders as she lost herself in the age-old rhythm.

When it was over he collapsed, the conquering strength of a moment ago gone as if it had never existed. Tiffany lay, almost bewildered, accepting the weight of his body without demur. Her heart thundered in her chest; she could feel the hammer strokes making a wild rhythm of their own with Eliot's. She should be angry. Later she would be. But at the moment she could only feel a kind of sensual satiety which rendered her incapable of anything but astonishment.

Then Eliot moved, and released from his weight she realised what had happened. And turned on to her stomach, hiding her face in the pillows in an access of shame and humiliation.

'Why?'

When she refused to answer he dragged her over on to her back so ungently that tears of pain glittered beneath her lashes. He was pale and there was a white line around his mouth as he demanded again with harsh distinctness, 'Why? What the hell has been going on?'

Tiffany could not face the incandescent blaze of his gaze. She closed her eyes against him, pressing her lips together to prevent them from trembling. She was sore, her skin painful as though she had been whipped, but greater than the physical pain was her mental torment.

His voice altered, became less urgent as he regained some control. 'Tiffany, why didn't you tell me?'

'Why should I?' She opened her eyes, staring her defiance. 'I don't recall you ever asking. Would you have believed me even if I had? You—you were having far too much fun believing the worst of me. And it didn't ever occur to me that you would force me.'

'Christ,' he whispered, letting her go as if she were poisonous.

Oh, she had longed, *yearned* to see him topple from that pinnacle of arrogant self-assurance. Now it had happened and she was exhausted. For weeks she had been whipping up hatred to cover the urgent call of her body to his, afraid of it, resenting it. This final, cataclysmic scene was too much.

'Please go,' she said tiredly.

'Don't be bloody ridiculous.' He hauled the sheer over her with an absent gesture which revealed just how often he had shared a bed before. His hand trembled. He held it away from him, staring at it, then burst out, '*God!* You stupid little fool, didn't you know that this was inevitable? Naïve as you are, you must have felt the attraction. You were ready for me—you must have known that I wanted you.'

'Oh yes, I knew,' she said in a remote little voice. 'As for being naïve—well, yes, I suppose I was. I thought I could trust you. So yes, I am naïve. And stupid.'

'Oh God, it figures.' His voice was tired, heavy with self-disgust and anger. Without looking at her he rolled over on to his stomach, turning his head away. The dark hair was ruffled and damp. Tiffany remembered the springy vitality of it beneath her fingers and colour drenched her skin in a bitter realisation of just how much she had co-operated in her own rape.

But even as defeat, acrid and painful, clogged her throat, her eyes drifted across the broad plane of his shoulders. And she had to clench hands which could still feel the smooth skin stretched tight over muscles bunched in a tension he must have felt many times before.

Join the club, she thought, fighting the tingle of desire in the pit of her stomach. You are now one of Eliot Buchanan's women.

'OK,' he said, as he brought his arms up to form a cradle for his head. 'We'll have to get married. Hell, what a joke! Caught by a half-witted virgin without the sense to know what time of day it is! When can you be ready?'

Twice she tried to speak but the automatic functions of her body were suspended. When her voice appeared it was thin and angry. 'Don't be a fool.'

'Why?' This brought his head around. Something smouldering in the depths of his eyes warned her to be careful. He looked as though he could kill her.

'Why?' he asked again, adding curtly, 'I don't go around seducing virgins, you know. It's not my style.'

'Well, you just have,' she retorted, acid anger overriding caution. 'And as there is absolutely no way I'll marry you you're just going to have to learn to live with yourself. I can't think of anyone I'd like to marry less.'

For the second time in a few minutes she had the immense satisfaction of seeing him knocked off that autocratic mountain peak he occupied.

'Really?' he asked silkily, lifting himself up on an elbow. His mouth thinned when she jerked the sheet up to hold it beneath her chin, staring at him with great, unfriendly eyes.

'Really,' she emphasised. Surprisingly, her voice was quite steady. She sounded almost normal. She was vaguely pleased by this when her composure was shattered by his next comment, delivered in his smoothest, most dangerous voice.

'Why not? We've just discovered that we match very nicely in the most basic way of all. For a virgin you display a gratifying amount of passion; I think I could become addicted to those gasping little moans you give and the way your hands search out my most sensitive parts. You're a natural, Tiffany, born for sex.'

His long fingers drifted up and began to stroke the soft swell of her breasts beneath the sheet. Gasping as much with outrage as with the sensations those clever, experienced fingers were producing she pushed the hand away but the fine cotton was too revealing.

'See?' he said hatefully, smiling down at the tiny nub his skilful fingers had coaxed forth.

'Are you planning a marriage that's one long orgy?' she asked furiously.

He grinned unpleasantly and bent his head, catching the nipple in his teeth. Tiffany stiffened and tried to push his head away. He laughed and opened his mouth on to her breast. The cotton sheet was no protection. She felt the damp moistness as if it was a brand and was appalled by the sudden heat of passion which roared in her ears.

'That's not a bad idea,' he said mockingly, resisting her efforts to free herself.

'It's a very bad idea. I'm not—I won't——' She was flustered, unable to breathe or to think. His laughter was rough in her ears as he lifted his head to kiss the junction where her neck met her shoulder. She turned her head away in dumb defiance, trying desperately to make her brain think. His mouth was warm and persuasive.

'You are and you will,' he said tormenting her with the amusement in his voice. 'You enjoyed making love with me as much as I enjoyed taking you. Didn't you, Tiffany?' And when she shook her head he laughed again, his breath warm against her skin. 'Shall I make you admit it? I could, quite easily, couldn't I? You weren't faking when you welcomed me so ardently into your body. You wanted me, you said so, again and again and again, in that sultry, throaty little voice, and you were just about insane with it. I could sense it, and it drove me mad . . .'

'*No!*'

Forgetting modesty she shot out of the bed and made for the wardrobe, grabbing her dressing-gown. Eliot gave a low, satisfied laugh as he lay back against the pillows, his hands locked together behind his dark head, smiling.

Like some—some oriental potentate watching a favourite slave girl, she thought, anger making her fumble as she hauled the dressing-gown on over her nakedness.

He looked totally in command, very pleased with himself and completely confident of his power over her. Conceited swine!

'We have nothing in common,' she bit out.

'If you think that, you're not only naïve, you're an idiot.' He shrugged at the scorching glare she threw him. 'Sexually we go together like strawberries and cream. Oh, come on, Tiffany, pull your head out of the sand for long enough to admit that. I knew we would be. That's been the trouble. The first time I saw you I knew that you'd be a wild little devil in bed and every time I touched you or came near you I felt a response which told me I could have you.'

'You're so smug,' she spat shakily. 'Have me? You didn't have, you took. I *despise* you.'

'After the first minute or so I didn't notice much resistance,' he said nastily. 'That's why it didn't occur to me that you were a virgin. Hell, you went up in flames. If I took, so did you, and if that makes me a lecher without any redeeming features, where does it leave you? The female equivalent, that's where. I wasn't imagining things when you writhed and twisted against me, pleading with me——'

'Shut up!' she blazed, cutting his insolent words short.

When he flung back the sheets she whirled, hands over her ears and eyes tight shut to hide his splendid nakedness.

From behind her he said maliciously, 'If I treated you as a sex object, Tiffany, you did exactly the same to me. In my book that makes us even. Or are you going to tell me that beneath the hatred and the chagrin you're really in love with me?'

'Don't be an *idiot*.' Her voice shook with frustration and rage. 'I loathe you. You must be mad to think that I'd appease your guilt by marrying you just because you think we're compatible in one area.'

'But a most important one,' he said with cool persistence. 'Besides, there's something else I've just thought of. You never bore me.'

'Oh!' She flung around, hands crooked into claws and went scarlet again. 'Will you go and put your clothes on, for heaven's sake. I can't—I won't talk to you like that.'

He flung his head back, totally unselfconscious as laughter shook his chest. Tiffany's mouth dried as she looked up at his arrogant, well-defined features, caught again in a sensual aura which enveloped her and held her fast.

Her heart began to thud in her breast, slow heavy strokes which picked up speed as he stopped laughing and looked into her wide eyes. The muscles in her throat moved; she swallowed, caught in the blazing heat of his gaze. Her tongue touched her lips. His eyes fastenedn to it, narrowed, intent.

'Yes,' he said softly, all amusement fled. In the strong lines of his throat a pulse beat. He reached out and took her hand and held it against his chest. Her fingers splayed, rigid, and then relaxed against the hard wall, his life-beat thundering against her palm.

He mouth formed the word no, but soundlessly, and when he pulled her close to him she did not resist. But when she looked up at him the triumph in his expression jerked her free of his arms and she shouted, '*No!* I won't be——'

'Seduced?'

'. . . coerced into anything.' She floundered then caught her breath. 'Not bed, not marriage, not *anything*. Will you get out of here?'

'For the time being, yes.' Long, strong fingers slid around her throat, daring her to move. 'I know what's the matter,' he said, smiling mirthlessly into her defiant face. 'You've just discovered the difference between your romantic ideals and the crude reality of life, and you're fighting a desperate rearguard action. I'll go now, but I'll be back. And when I am you'd better have made up your mind to opt for reality. After all, you could be pregnant with my child.'

As a parting shot it couldn't have been bettered. Numbly Tiffany sank down on to a chair and sat with face averted while faint noises revealed that he was dressing. When he came across to her she held herself rigidly still, hating him, dreading his power to make her forget just how much she hated him.

'Try not to worry too much,' he said, very much the lawyer, totally in command. 'I'll be in touch soon.'

To breathe hurt but she managed, dragging air into lungs too long denied. 'Don't bother,' she retorted, trying to emulate the crispness of his tones. 'I meant what I said. Just leave me alone.'

'Sometimes I think a beating would do you the world of good.'

'You try it and see where it gets you.'

Tension jagged through the silent moments but she refused to look at him. After a short pause he said off-handedly, 'Very well then, wallow in self-pity if you must. I hope that you'll be in a more rational mood when I see you next.'

She heard his footsteps, light for a man of his size and strength. At the bottom of the stairs he said something to Jess and then the door slammed.

The tears didn't come until she heard the sound of his car die away down the road. But his stinging comment about self-pity prevented too long an indulgence. When the bout had brought its inevitable conclusion, a headache and sore eyes, she showered and washed her hair before stripping the bed and remaking it. By then it was late enough to go to bed. She settled Jess down, made herself some hot milk and took an aspirin with it before lying awake for hours wondering just how she was ever going to convince Eliot that she was not going to marry him.

From there her thoughts drifted to his shock when he had discovered that she was a virgin. He had been so astounded that he hadn't even bothered to ask her why Geoffrey had left her such a large chunk of his estate if it wasn't for services rendered. She could not hope for immunity from questions when next they met. By then he would have recovered his self-possession and he would use all of his legal skills to force some sort of answer from her.

Not that he would get one. If she refused point blank to provide him with reasons for Geoffrey's actions there was nothing he could do to make her talk.

Even at the height of their mutual ecstasy she had not—would not have—told him. Slowly, without volition, her hand touched her heart. They had made love in a heat of passion, everything else stifled but the hunger which had overpowered them both. And when their bodies had merged into union she had cried out, not really with pain but because she had known in that moment that this was what she had been born for. The sensations which had exploded into rapture had been so far removed from any fantasy she had ever had that she smiled now, thinking of the Tiffany Brandon who had never known what it was like to lie in Eliot's arms, to love him . . .

No! Not to love him, never to love him. Love was gentle and kind, it was a sharing, a giving. What she felt for Eliot was a wild amalgam of fascination and desire and hatred and the only thing she wanted from him was the satisfaction of the physical hunger he roused in her.

It was the same for him. He had set out to humiliate her and within minutes he had cast aside all restraint, intent only on losing himself in that enchantment of the senses, using her with a tenderness which had been a cruelty in itself. And in those final moments of cataclysm it had been love words he had whispered into her hair, endearments forced from him because the sensual magic between them could only be expressed that way.

This power they possessed over each other was perilously close to love and every bit as strong. It hurt as much, it was just as binding while it lasted, but it was not going to strengthen and deepen as love did. In time it would pass. She must never forget that.

Lines from a dead poet came to her mind. She had never consciously learned them but they surfaced now, hauled up from the depths of her memory:

> Ask nothing more of me, sweet;
> All I can give you I give . . .

And that, she told herself with brutal realism, that was taking, that was not giving. Oh, he had enjoyed her, the contempt he felt swamped by his desire. For those long minutes when he had made himself master of her responses, forcing her into a ravishment of the senses which was purely physical, she had been the most important person in his world.

But only for those moments, and she would do well to remember that, for him, there had been other women. In the future there would be more. Any woman who was young and nubile and reasonably attractive—and available—would be able to produce that look of agonised ecstasy which had tightened the skin over the framework of his face so that the cold austerity of it had been transformed. Probably, she decided, rubbing the truth in, when he was making love was the only time in his life that he ever lost control. Then, he was completely at the mercy of the primitive urges and needs which fuel all of our drives, those remnants of our barbarous past over which the fabric of civilisation stretches so thinly.

But that didn't explain why he had almost forced her. She knew, and didn't even wonder how she knew, that he would not normally have persisted in the face of her attempt to deny him. Although his aura of sexuality was so potent that he could probably have almost any woman he wanted there must have been times when he had been refused. He was essentially civilised so his reaction to a rebuff would be civilised, too. But of course, things were not like that between them. They were linked by bonds almost as strong as the bonds of love, for they hated each other and the very power of their emotions, based as they were on a kind of desire she did not understand, was a potent aphrodisiac.

He had used his masculine strength to subdue her in the most basic fashion. Another man might have beaten her but Eliot had made love to her, forcing her to accept her own sensuality, to realise that this man she loathed could coax her body into a surrender which had been a dark victory and a defeat for them both.

So now she loathed and feared him. And liked him, for he had been kind to her.

Lying there in the bed in which he had taken her she shivered, suddenly swept by pain and a longing which was pain too. That was the danger—the longing, the desire which had its roots in some kind of physical hunger over which no one had any control. Yet she would have to learn to subdue the pleadings of her body even if she could do nothing about the basic attraction. Because if she gave in to it she would end up used and discarded. That way lay self-contempt and bitter distrust and an anguish of mind which she only dimly foresaw.

So when the doorbell rang the next day she was glad that she was upstairs, glad that she managed to grab Jess before she could bark her usual warning. A quick glance through the window revealed the Lotus. Hands clamped around the dog's muzzle, Tiffany stood barely breathing, hoping that he would take the hint and go away.

The bell pealed several times more before quick footsteps on the path made her relax and sigh her relief. Not for long, however.

Mrs Crowe's voice came clear, and all too interested. 'Good morning, Mr Buchanan. Lovely day, isn't it?'

'Beautiful. Tell me, have you seen Miss Brandon go out?'

Mrs Crowe answered innocently, 'Why, no. She took Jessie for a walk this morning, but I'm sure she's at home now. She doesn't go out much, you know.'

'I know.' Some note entered his voice. Upstairs, rigid with fury, Tiffany recognised it as one of satisfaction.

His voice came louder and more clearly. 'She wasn't very well when I left her yesterday. I wonder if she . . .'

'Oh, do you think she might be ill again?' All too easily persuaded, Mrs Crowe sounded worried. 'What do you think we should do?'

'I could pick the lock,' Eliot suggested outrageously, 'or perhaps—no, I don't think we should contact the police. Yet. If I get in, do you think you——'

'Oh, yes, of course. It takes quite a few weeks to recover from some of the viruses we get now, doesn't it. She might have had a relapse, poor child.'

Gritting her teeth, Tiffany realised that Eliot was giving her no chance to avoid him. She wouldn't even put it past him to call the police. Wondering angrily why he had this need to dominate she put Jess down just as the doorbell rang again.

'Ah, you are in.' His vivid blue gaze was bland and coldly amused.

'Are you all right?' Mrs Crowe sounded quite alarmed. 'We were beginning to worry.'

Tiffany managed to smile as she disclaimed any signs of illness. 'I didn't hear the bell,' she lied before asking her neighbour in for tea.

'No, my dear, much as I'd like to.' Mrs Crowe was arch, her twinkling glance moving from Tiffany to Eliot in a way which showed just how her thoughts were running. 'I'm going out soon, and there are still a few things to do.'

Which left Eliot, who was accepting Jess's greetings with his usual aplomb. When he straightened up he looked Tiffany over, his gaze lingering on her mouth which was still slightly swollen from the passion of his kisses.

'Don't ever do that again,' he said with icy distinctness. 'I'm quite competent at lock-picking if I have to.'

'Why can't you understand? I don't want to see you.'

His smile was pure irony, remorseless and persistent. 'I spent a considerable amount of last night thinking.'

'Oh.' Tiffany felt the hairs on the back of her neck lift. Uneasily she watched as he strolled across to the sofa and sat down. He smiled again.

'Yes. Come and join me, Tiffany.'

Cold fear had kept her still. Wincing at that unpleasant smile she forced herself to walk over to the chair. Her eyes were hot and dry. She wanted to blink but she had the strange feeling that if she did she would give him an advantage. So she stared at him, her lips pressed tightly together to prevent them from trembling.

He was impossibly arrogant, holding her eyes with a sardonic amusement which covered other, darker emotions. Beneath that formidable self-possession he was angry.

'Clever Tiffany—or perhaps I should call you Tifaine. It's a pretty name, isn't it? Unusual too,' he mocked, watching her through half-closed eyes as she blinked in shock. 'French, I'm told. Shall I tell you what I've decided about you?'

'Can I stop you?'

'No.' But he was in no hurry to begin. He was enjoying this moment of power.

When he did speak it was with a sudden return to his brisk, emotionless lawyer's manner. 'I was surprised by Geoffrey's bequest to you. When I suggested that you would prefer money he was quite adamant that his grandmother's jewels should go to you. I wondered why, as she was about the only person I ever knew Geoffrey to be sentimental about. However, they were worth very little, and as Diane would certainly sell them I decided that he'd probably promised you jewellery and that these were a sop to your greed. It niggled, however. Enough for me to institute a search for your birth certificate.'

'But—that's illegal!'

'It's not. I had no intention of using it for any illegal purpose. When I got home last night it was in the mail. Your mother's name was there, all right, but there was a rather betraying gap where the father's should have been. And your first name was very definitely Tifaine. By a strange—coincidence—that happens to have been Geoffrey's grandmother's name. Interested?'

'I'm sure you can't wait to tell me,' she said tightly, then bit her lip.

Still in that remorseless, judicial voice he continued, 'So I had a short talk with my mother. She has an excellent memory. After a little prompting she remembered that some twenty or so years ago Geoffrey had a secretary called Marie Brandon. Altogether too many coincidences to be believable, don't you agree?'

Tiffany said nothing.

'She—this secretary—was a very attractive, quiet woman. Geoffrey's wife conceived a bitter jealousy for her; she was inclined to do that sort of thing, I'm afraid. However, in this case she made Geoffrey's life hideous until finally he got rid of his secretary. My mother remembered it vividly because my aunt Margaret was even less balanced than normal about this Marie Brandon. One can see that she had reason.'

'Congratulations,' she said woodenly. 'What do you do for an encore? And what do you want?'

'You,' he told her with quiet malice. When she stared numbly at him he smiled and rose and came across to pull her out of the chair, his fingers on her wrist tightening in momentary cruelty as she made to jerk free. 'Why the blush? You know that I want you.'

'Last night——' Her colour deepened but she went steadily on. 'Last night it was in anger.'

'You really are an innocent, aren't you?' He sounded almost shaken. 'Oh, I was angry. Furious. But I made love to you because ever since I first saw a little provincial flirting lightly with my uncle, I've starved for you. I despised myself for being so weak but even though I believed that you were nothing but a cheap little tease, using youth and a meretricious freshness to ensnare an old man, I couldn't get you out of my brain. Or my blood.'

His words hurt, the more because there was a note beneath the careful steadiness which revealed how it angered him to admit what he saw as a weakness.

'Even if I was—what you thought,' she said huskily, 'you had no right to do what you did.'

'Do you think I don't know that?' He hesitated. His fingers slid from the small fine bones of her wrist to enclose her hand, holding it in a firm grip. When he spoke it was in level tones, restrained and cool.

'I've told you I'm sorry,' he began, then stopped at her choked little laugh. 'What is it?'

'When? You didn't offer me any apology. You were furious because I'd dared to be a virgin. Then you nobly offered to marry me. But I don't recall that you said you were sorry.'

'Come and sit down.' He waited until they were seated side by side before he fitted wide shoulders into the back of the sofa. He had relinquished her hand.

When he spoke he steepled his own together, watching them.

'Then I'm sorry for that too,' he said gravely.

Tiffany was very still, her whole being concentrated on him. The apology was sincere but she knew, some female instinct told her, that what he regretted most was not the effect his behaviour had had on her. He still resented her; it was there in the note of impatience in his voice. She knew why, too. During the time she had known him she had begun to understand him, to perceive the salient points of his personality. It was impossible to listen to anyone talk on subjects they have views about and not become aware of their thoughts and feelings, the skeleton of beliefs and attitudes which underpins their words and actions.

During those evenings when he and Geoffrey had talked she had soaked it all in. His conversation, his sense of humour, even the changing expressions of his face, became her map to his character. He revealed less of himself than most men, but she had watched and listened and absorbed, not realising that she was fascinated by him.

And she had learnt that one of the qualities he admired, found desirable and necessary, was self-control. For him it was one of the corner-stones of a well adjusted life.

Which was why he was sitting beside her now, resenting her. Because whatever had happened last night, whether he had taken her in lust or anger or passion, he had taken her because he totally lost control. The darker emotions hidden by sophistication had been let loose in a conflagration and for that he blamed her.

His apology was a sop to his conscience, just as his proposal was to his honour. He must, she thought drearily, believe her to be half-witted as well as basically untrustworthy.

'Tiffany?'

She shivered and turned her head to look at him.

'Oh, I accept your apology,' she said drily. 'But I'm not going to marry you, Eliot. As you promised me last night, what we did was not rape.'

'It was seduction, which is as bad.'

She smiled ironically. 'It's a bit late to be developing a conscience about it. Whatever it was, it's no basis for marriage.'

He was not going to plead, or even argue with her, but her adamant refusal both surprised and angered him. Eliot, it was easy to see, had very rarely been refused. And when it was a proposal of marriage—well, she understood. In a way he was spoilt. No doubt there had been many women who had yearned to be his wife. He was not to be blamed if he thought it an honour.

But although she found herself thinking of reasons why she should give in, pride and hard common sense made it impossible.

'And that's your last word, is it?'

She nodded. 'It would never work,' she said soberly. 'When I marry I intend it to be forever. We're not in love—what sort of marriage would that be?'

'The sort almost every other culture considers normal,' he said.

Tiffany looked up at him but there was nothing to be read in his expression. The mask was firmly back in place. Even the vivid brilliance of his eyes was darkened and there was a hard disciplined line to his mouth. He looked like a bronze god, almost impassive yet dynamically charged with power.

Mouth dry she said, 'I think you'd better go.'

And he went.

After she had closed the door behind him Tiffany stood for a long time staring across the room, her eyes dark smudges above a mouth suddenly red and trembling.

He wanted too much. She had caught the possessive look he had given her as he left. Colour ran through her skin as recollections of his passion and her wild surrender came to her. They did not love: what he felt was a hungry need to subdue. Like her, he was in thrall to a sexual need so great that will-power only succeeded in restraining the open expression of it, leaving the hidden obsession gnawing at the fabric of their lives.

He had spoken the truth when he said that he had wanted her from that first sighting. It had been reciprocal but she had been too inexperienced to realise that her anger and dislike had been so great because it was rooted in a strong awareness, an enslavement of the senses.

There could be no future for them. When this madness had faded, as fade it must, they would be left with the empty husk of a dead desire and they would tear each other apart.

Before she went to bed that night Tiffany sat by the window and watched the silver tears of rain streaking the pane. Jess snuffled and twitched, lost in some canine dream. The wind cried softly.

Slowly Tiffany's resolve hardened into certainty. What Eliot wanted was her complete capitulation. An instinct of domination bred in him made it impossible for him to accept that the only true marriage was one held together by love and trust and desire. Any future together must see them as equals, differentiated only by the fact that she was female and he male. If he could not understand that she needed his acceptance of this as much as she needed him, then there was no future.

She did not ask herself why she was making conditions for a future for them both. She still saw him only as a man who fascinated her, body and mind. The word love did not once enter her head.

CHAPTER SIX

HE did not come near her for over ten days. She had not expected him to. What had happened had been as much a shock to him as it had to her. Not only did he have to come to terms with his own loss of control but with her refusal of his proposal. It would be a bitter time for him.

So she sewed and missed him with a heavy ache in her heart, and told herself that if she never saw him again she would be in luck.

One wet day she delivered a parcel of goods to a shop in Remuera and was walking quickly back to the bus stop, avoiding as well as she could the maniacs who seemed incapable of managing their umbrellas. It had been raining for several hours and the gutters were running full. Everyone wore harassed expressions except for one small boy in a pair of bright yellow gumboots who stamped gleefully in every puddle he could find. His mother had the look of one who has given up trying, but when Tiffany's laughing glance met her eyes she grinned back.

It was a momentary little incident but it warmed Tiffany's heart, giving her cheeks a glow that had been missing for some time. It was just then that a hand slid beneath her elbow and Eliot said in her ear, 'If you marry me you can have a son like that.'

Sheer shock robbed her of any speech. She twisted her head to look up at him, her heart contracting as she saw the signs of his frustration. His features were sharper, his smile edgy, and his eyes had lost the vivid colour which made them so conspicuous.

'I told you,' she began, but he lifted his hand and laid a finger across her lips, shaking his head.

'How you do go on,' he complained. 'Come and have lunch with me.'

'Eliot——'

'No strings. Just a pleasant meal, in pleasant surroundings with a pleasant companion.'

She should have said no, but her hungry heart overrode the promptings of her common sense.

'Well—I suppose . . .'

'Don't force yourself,' he said brusquely, that brief moment of pleading gone.

She smiled, she couldn't help herself. 'Oh, you're quite impossible!'

'And so,' he said deliberately, 'are you. Unfortunately. Impossible to forget.'

'Have you been trying?'

'Yes, Oh, yes, very hard.' His fingers gripped her arm, preventing her instinctive attempt to free herself. 'No, you've agreed to eat with me. Let's pretend that we've only just met each other. We'll be very polite but very interested in each other and I'll show you that I can behave with perfect propriety.'

She smiled a little ironically at this, but in such a mood he was very endearing. 'I've never doubted that,' she said calmly.

'Haven't you? I'm surprised. I've hardly behaved to you with any sort of propriety.'

'I thought we were going to forget about that.'

He smiled down into her flushed face, deliberately using that charm he must find so useful. 'Of course. Do you know that when you are—aroused—your eyes glitter with tiny gold sparks? And you have an enchanting way of lifting your lashes slowly which drives me mad.' His hand slid down towards her wrist, his thumb finding the blue veins there before his fingers grasped hers.

'For someone who—whom I've only just met, you're very—personal,' Tiffany said, trying very hard to make her voice as even as it normally was.

He laughed, and squeezed her hand, 'I am notorious for my flirtatious manner,' he said solemnly. 'A very fast worker when I see something I want. And although we've only just met I've discovered that I want you.'

Oh, he was hopeless! It was as though all of the bitterness and extravagent emotion had never been. Over lunch he teased her and laughed with her, treating her as if she was something fragile and precious to him, making unashamed use of his charm to coax her into a response which astonished her. In this mood he was irresistible and he knew it and played on her helpless response.

Afterwards he took her home in spite of her protests, asking as he opened the door, 'Are you going to ask me in?'

'No,' she said solemnly. 'I don't know you well enough for that.'

Something in the glitter in his eyes promised retribution but he hid it quickly and said with light emphasis, 'Then we'll have to change that,' and picked up her hand and kissed it, first on the wrist and then, his narrowed eyes gleaming as they scanned her flushed face, the palm. His mouth was warm but what made her heart leap—and her body shout its awareness—was the light touch of his tongue on the sensitive skin.

'Au revoir,' he said blandly, and left her.

That night he rang to ask if she would like to go to dinner and a film. She stumbled and hesitated and he said coolly, 'I'll pick you up tomorrow night at six then,' and rang off before she had time to tell him that she didn't want to go anywhere with him.

It would have been a lie but she should have forced it out, because her heart thumped and she later found herself dreaming of him—and the dream was not the sort one would look up in a dream book. So explicit was it that she woke moaning in a fever of excited desire, only to find herself whimpering with frustration as the truth forced itself coldly on her.

By morning the rain had cleared away leaving the city sparkling beneath a sky so burnished and blue that the islands of the gulf were cut-out shapes against the glittering sea and the horizon. After Jess's walk Tiffany sewed fiercely, concentrating so hard that by five o'clock she had given herself a headache.

A bath rid her of it, but the bruised look smudged her eyes as she applied eye shadow carefully and tried to bring some order to her curls. It was a useless task, as it had been from early childhood. She flicked a comb through her hair and left it. It was hopeless trying to look even the slightest bit sophisticated with that bubbly frame around her face. The dress she chose was one her mother had made for her; all that afternoon she had had to restrain her compulsion to rush out and buy something more elegant and up-market. Not that there was anything wrong with what she had on now. Marie had excellent taste and was as skilful at a sewing machine as her daughter.

The deep rust-red of the dress emphasised her colouring, lending warmth to her skin. The white asymmetrical collar and cuffs gave it a schoolgirlish air, as did the buttons up the front, emphasised by four rows of tucks. Or so she thought as she slipped on black shoes and sprayed herself with 'Miss Dior'. The dress skimmed from the shoulders to a dropped waist and then fell in soft pleats to just below her knees. It revealed very little of the body beneath, save that it was young and supple.

'Making a point?' Eliot murmured as he held the door open for you. 'You look like someone's kid sister.'

'Disappointed?'

He met the suddenly tilted jaw and challenging stare with amusement and a challenge of his own. 'No, my sweet, I'm not in the least disappointed. I dislike the obvious.'

'Even when you fall into that trap yourself?'

He didn't pretend not to know what she was talking about. 'No,' he said calmly. 'I didn't *dislike* that. I felt murderous. As you may have noticed.'

'I did indeed,' she murmured, unable to prevent herself from shivering.

Instead of immediately starting the car he sat with his hands on the wheel and stared down at the strong fingers while he asked, 'Tiffany, are you pregnant?'

'I—I don't know.' Shaken by his unexpected question her voice quavered before firming. 'I'll know in about ten days.'

'I see.' A long pause, heavy with unspoken tension, and then he resumed, 'Will you promise to tell me the truth?'

Nervously her teeth clamped on to her bottom lip. 'Yes,' she said huskily and could not prevent herself from asking, 'Why?'

'Because I am not like Geoffrey. I have no intention of allowing any child of mine to grow up without knowing me.' He spoke evenly, without any emotion in the deep voice. 'So if you had any ideas about skipping off, forget it. I'd find you, and I wouldn't be pleased. I may not be your idea of a good husband but I have every intention of being an excellent father.'

'I see.' Something painful and hard lodged in her throat. As he switched the engine and the lights on she turned her head slightly so that she could just see the clean, hard line of his profile against the subdued city light outside. It looked totally determined, a ruthless outline. He was a man who wore his character in his face. And did that last speech mean that he had given up the idea of marrying her? Tiffany told herself stoutly that she hoped that he had, ignoring the empty feeling in the pit of her stomach. Her refusal to marry him had astonished as well as angered him. Eliot was not used to rejection of any sort. But that cold, logical brain must have forced him to realise that a marriage like the one he had suggested could never work.

No doubt, she decided, savagely thinking the worst, this latest development was just to keep her sweet until she knew for certain whether or not she was pregnant. If she wasn't he would suggest his usual arrangement, whatever that was. Dinner, bed and breakfast three times a week? If she was—well, even her fertile imagination boggled at the thought of Eliot as an unmarried father.

To banish the dismal visions her brain conjured up she asked on an indrawn breath, 'Where are we going?'

'Oh, a small restaurant. The food's good and it's close to the cinema.'

Her question marked the turning point of the evening. From then on he was exactly as he had been at lunch the day before, setting himself out to fascinate. He made her laugh, flirting smoothly with her across the table of the small but extremely exclusive restaurant. There was no hint of patronage in the deep voice when they discussed a political row which had blown up that day. Tiffany suppressed the warmth of satisfaction this gave her, just as she ignored the rather shamed pleasure she received from the envious looks of other people in the restaurant. Several of them came up to greet him; he introduced her but made it quite clear that he didn't want them lingering. And they all gave the same knowing smile, tempered by some astonishment, and moved on, leaving him with a clear field.

'They think you're trying to fix your interest,' she said, when the third couple moved on to their table. 'And they're surprised because I'm not your usual sort of woman. If only they knew the truth.'

'Which is?'

She shrugged, her eyes drawn against her will to his mouth. 'You know.'

'Yes, I know,' he said deliberately, 'but I doubt very much that you do.'

'I've never set myself up as a mind-reader,' she parried, picking up her wine glass to use as a shield against his scrutiny.

'Oh, I don't know,' he drawled, his smile edged with sharpness. 'You haven't done too badly in that respect. For a woman almost totally lacking in experience you have a surprisingly mature brain. And a rather frightening insight into other people's motives.'

Tiffany could have laughed at that. If she had had any insight into his motives she would have run screaming all the way back to the South Island the minute she had set eyes on him. 'Have you read Agatha Christie?' she asked.

He looked amused. 'Yes.'

'She had a detective, a fussy little old lady who lived in a small country village. Whenever she solved a murder she used to say that life in a village was every bit as grim and real and earthy as it was in the biggest cities in the world. Or words to that effect. And she was right. We might fail to understand the shibboleths and customs of your sophisticated circles, but when it comes to birth and death, jealousy and hatred and anger, well, we know all about those.'

The powerful shoulders moved slightly as though her words, delivered in a serenely judicial tone, had made him slightly uneasy. 'Knowledge is one thing,' he said abruptly. 'Experience is another. Have you finished?'

'Yes.'

'Then let's go.'

The film was good, a psychological drama which had strong overtones of terror so that at one stage Tiffany gasped and clutched Eliot's sleeve. Even in the dimness of the cinema she could see the white flash of his smile as he took her hand in his and held it until the final, shattering climax.

It was raining again when they came out into the night, not heavily but with a thin persistence which boded ill for the morrow. Eliot tucked her hand in his arm and hurried her across the slick footpath towards the car. All down the street other cinemas were disgorging their patrons so that the pavement was crowded. An elderly woman slipped in a puddle, and fell, gasping. When her husband tried to help her to her feet she moaned and sank back, a hand on her ankle.

'I think I've sprained it,' she said to the small circle of people around her.

Within a minute, and without saying it openly, the group of people had offered the position of leader to Eliot and were busy doing what he told them. And a quarter of an hour after that both Eliot and Tiffany were waiting with the husband in the casualty ward at the hospital.

'This is very kind of you, Mr Buchanan,' the man said for the sixth or seventh time, his old eyes anxious as they scanned the door where his wife had been taken.

Eliot smiled, that rare, warm smile which made Tiffany's throat ache suddenly with a nameless emotion. 'Did you enjoy the film?'

'We did, indeed. And you, and your lady wife?'

'Very much,' Eliot said smoothly, daring Tiffany to object with one mocking, sideways glance. He had insisted on driving the elderly couple to the hospital and waiting with the worried husband while his wife was attended to. This was the obverse of his character, the gentler side he hid from most people as though he was ashamed of it. Yet he cared for this unknown couple as he had cared about Geoffrey, as he would care for his children. In a way his choice of profession was another instance of his concern for humanity.

An odd combination of cynicism and loving kindness, Tiffany reflected, before she set herself to diverting their companion's mind from his fears for his wife. Within a few minutes he was smiling and making use of a rather ponderous courtesy, so that when his wife appeared in a wheelchair he looked somewhat startled at the rapid passage of time.

'Just a sprain,' the doctor said cheerfully after an appreciative glance at Tiffany. 'I've bandaged it and given her some pills for any pain. See that she keeps off it as much as possible.'

The elderly couple were profuse in their thanks, even more profuse when Eliot made it clear that he intended to drive them home. Once there he carried Mrs Grainger into the house and set her down on her bed, smilingly refusing to be thanked or to stay for a cup of tea.

Back in the car he said nothing. Tiffany couldn't prevent herself from yawning. The windscreen wipers went swish, swish, swish, across the glass, hypnotic in their steady movement. Long silver needles of rain were aimed straight at them, heavy enough now for water to be running across the roads in glistening sheets. There wasn't much traffic and what little there was moved slowly and carefully. Staring at the rows and rows of houses with their coloured curtains glowing against the shadowed walls Tiffany wondered how many people were happy tonight, how many grieving, and, rather desperately, if anyone else in Auckland felt the same mixture of excitement and desolation as she did at this minute.

When the car engine faded she realised that she had been semi-asleep, only the seatbelt keeping her in place. Jerking herself upright she yawned again and Eliot said, half-laughing, 'Do you want me to carry you in, too?'

'No!' she exclaimed, and more slowly, 'no, thank you, I'm just tired.'

'A pity,' he said coolly, but was out of the car before she had time to snap back an answer.

As he always did he opened the door for her, but when she said her polite thanks he grinned rather wolfishly and said, 'Not quite so quickly, my sweet.'

But the kiss was light and teasing. Tiffany should have been glad but she sensed that this deliberate withholding was part of some strategy he had conceived. A little flame of anger made her reckless. She slid her arms around his neck and pressed a kiss into the warmth of his neck, making sure that her body rested against his for a split-second before she withdrew and slammed the door.

Within a few seconds the engine started and the car's wheels sang as they gripped the tarmac. Tiffany let out a deep breath and straightened up from the door. That had been stupid. That had been a deliberate provocation, a challenge to his masculinity, and Eliot had already shown her how he reacted to a challenge.

'Your mistress has been an idiot,' she told Jess wryly, 'but it won't happen again, I promise.'

Easily enough said, the decision. And in the long darkness of her sleepless night it had to be the most sensible decision she could make.

When he rang at nine the next night and invited her out at the weekend she said with only a momentary hesitation, 'No, Eliot, thank you but I think it would be better not to——'

'Do you?' The implacable note she hated hardened in his voice. 'I don't, and if you're not ready I'll soon see that you are, if I have to dress you myself.'

'You wouldn't dare,' she said thinly.

'Do you really think not?'

A wave of icy realisation chilled her skin. 'This is silly,' she began forcefully, only to be interrupted again.

'I know,' he said sympathetically. 'Which is why you are going to be dressed in your best by seven-thirty and waiting for me. Because if you aren't I shall take you up to your bedroom and strip you systematically and throughly. And then we might get there or we might not. OK?'

'I hate you,' she said, eradicating the tremble in her voice by sheer force of will.

He laughed. 'I know, darling. Such an exciting hatred, isn't it? See you Saturday.'

When she had slammed the receiver down she stood looking at her hands with a kind of detached fatalism. They were trembling. She didn't know whether it was because she hated him, or because when he threatened her his voice had been impregnated with a kind of stark sensuality which caused her body to prickle with sensations she could still feel.

'I hate him,' she whispered and picked Jess up and buried her face in the dog's fur.

She was ready, of course. As she stared at her reflection in the mirror she admitted that it was because she wanted to be with him. And wondering wearily why her resistance was so weak she pushed a wayward curl back behind her ears.

This time she had succumbed to temptation and bought herself a blouse of immensely romantic style in cream silk and handmade lace to wear with a black skirt which swished elegantly around her legs. A belt emphasised her narrow waist; with it she wore some of her great-grandmother's jewellery, a garnet and seed-pearl ring with earrings to match.

It did not need the quick flame of appreciation in Eliot's gaze to tell her that she looked good.

'Timeless,' he said with a note of mockery in his voice.

Her head came up into a defiant tilt. 'Where are we going?'

'You look perfect for anything.'

This time the mockery was in her expression. 'Flattery, Eliot?'

'Don't you know the truth when you hear it?' His voice hardened as he looked her over with deliberate insolence. 'Perfect. Serene, sweet, elegantly composed with a hint of demure, Victorian innocence. Oh, you'll be a riot tonight.'

'Where—are—we—going?' She spoke as if he was a half-wit and she trying to teach him something difficult. His sardonic appraisal made her skin prickle with outrage yet beneath the anger there was a queer, breathless excitement and just for a moment she remembered how his hands and mouth had mapped the contours of her body until all thoughts of resistance had fled in a turmoil of sensation such as she had never imagined.

Colour flamed along her cheekbones as she thrust the disturbing recollection from her. She didn't trust Eliot. Tonight she would need all of her wits. The dissipation of them in erotic memories was an indulgence she couldn't afford.

'Wait and see,' he told her coolly and when she refused to move he took her by the wrist and pulled her towards him. 'We could, of course, always stay here,' he threatened softly, smiling into her angry face.

'I despise you.'

'I know. Unfortunate that you also want me, isn't it? Now, are you coming or shall we make ourselves comfortable here?'

'Do you always descend to threats to get your own way?' she demanded, allowing herself to be ushered towards the door.

'Invariably. It saves a lot of arguing and waste of time.'

A smile pulled at the corner of her mouth. He was quite impossible. And whatever game he was playing was a kind of delicious torture for her, one that she was almost willing to accept. *Almost* willing? As the car purred into motion her smile became rueful. She was only too willing to let him bully her because she was miserable away from him.

She was not nearly so sanguine some twenty minutes later when he turned into the driveway of a large house at Kohimarama, one of Auckland's prestige seaside suburbs.

'A private party?' she asked thinly.

'Friends of mine. You'll like Alex and Christabel.' The engine was switched off; he turned his head and looked at her tense profile. 'Relax, Tiffany. No one is going to eat you.'

No, they didn't do that, and she did like Christabel Thomassin and her tall, handsome husband, but she would have been completely without intelligance not to have realised within five minutes that they moved in a social circle far more sophisticated than any she had ever imagined. Alex Thomassin was an Australian, a dark, handsome, positive man who shared with Eliot that total self-confidence which belongs only to the very rich. His wife, tall and exquisite, had been a model, so Eliot told Tiffany, and it was easy to see that they were totally absorbed in each other. Tiffany found herself fighting a nasty little niggle of envy. It wasn't fair for two people to have everything when it seemed that she was going to miss out on what she wanted most of all.

However she wasn't going to let herself be intimidated by the roomful of beautiful people, most of whom knew exactly who she was. She had not been so interested by her hosts that she did not realise that there were knowing smiles behind the social greetings or that she and Eliot were providing a fascinating topic of conversation to quite a few people.

'You're looking fierce,' he said quietly into her ear. 'I thought that I was the only person who caused that particular expression. What is it?'

She didn't know whether he had brought her here as a test to see whether she could cope with an occasion like this, or whether he was flaunting her as his next mistress. The latter, probably. Lifting her head to smile at him with deliberate, taunting provocation she said, 'Do you like having half the people here gossiping about us?'

Something ugly glittered beneath his lashes before his lids came down to hide it. 'Gossip doesn't worry me,' he said indifferently. His glance swept the room with a calm lack of interest. 'As for this lot—well, Alex and Christabel are the only two worth knowing here. I thought you might find that you had a lot in common with her.'

She stared in bewilderment. 'Why? She's absolutely gorgeous.'

'You have this crushing great inferiority complex,' he drawled smoothly, taking her hand and kissing the back of it with such *savoir faire* that he carried the gesture off perfectly. 'You must realise that you are far from plain yourself. Eyes like mountain pools, a mouth as fresh and kissable as a rose, and a body——' He grinned into her outraged face, winning a reluctant smile back from her. 'Well, perhaps I'd better wait until later to show you what I think of your body. It's not a subject I can hurry over.' And before she could protest at the ambiguity of his promise he continued, 'No, the reason I thought that you might enjoy Christabel's company is because you're both from the country. Christabel comes from the wilds of the far North.'

He had lifted his voice so that their hostess, who was coming towards them, couldn't help but hear him. She laughed and kissed his cheek. By far and away the tallest woman in the room, she made no concessions to her height, but even in the high heels she wore she was shorter than her husband and Eliot. Beside her Tiffany felt a midget.

'Isn't he a dreadful tease?' Christabel asked her indulgently. 'It's no wonder he and Alex get on so well. Demons, both of them. I left the far North when I was a child to spend most of my time in Australia's big cities.'

'Ah, but the North is your spiritual home,' her husband said, sliding an arm around her slender waist. He too smiled at Tiffany; she had the sudden feeling of being in a charmed circle. 'We're here to show our daughter off to her grandparents,' Alex added.

'And a little bit of business,' his wife teased, laughing.

After that it was a pleasant evening, made so because Tiffany found herself liking the Thomassins immensely. Christabel was a superb hostess but she found time to talk to Tiffany, bemusing her with her warmth.

'Eliot is a gorgeous man, isn't he?' she said, looking across the room to where he and her husband stood talking. 'He and Alex have been friends from way back. When I first met him I was terrified of him, he looked so austere and forbidding, but his wicked sense of humour soon put me at ease. He said that you haven't been here long—are you liking it?'

What followed was girl talk. Christabel was interested in Tiffany's work, saying with charming sincerity, 'You must be pleased to have found something you enjoy doing.' Christabel Thomassin possessed a charm so spontaneous and natural that its potency was unsuspected until it hit you.

The party ended shortly after midnight. After everyone else had left, Eliot and Tiffany stayed for coffee, and the conversation was pleasant and easygoing. Tiffany suspected that both Christabel and her handsome, dynamic husband were looking her over, but they hid the fact so cleverly that she relaxed, holding up her end of the conversation with a confidence which surprised her. Before they went home she was shown tiny Holly Thomassin, only three months old and obviously the joy of both her parents.

As if the party was some sort of signal, she found herself being invited to others, always with Eliot. She was frightened by this access of popularity but Eliot insisted on going and soon she began to know the people who made up his social circle. They were rich and attractive, most of them intelligent; she enjoyed their company but was wary, well aware that she was only there on sufferance. She discovered that Ella Sheridan was in America but was expected back soon. Occasionally she overheard people surmising about their relationship; it seemed to be generally accepted that she was his latest love.

Which was ironic, for although Eliot always kissed her good night, although he was a charming companion, making it quite obvious that he found her extremely attractive, he made no further attempt to make love to her. Those maddened minutes in her bed seemed never to have occurred.

Weeks went by and poor Tiffany, bewildered and out of her depth, went along with him. She told herself that it was because it was easier. But slowly, like a dreadful secret, she began to realise that, for her, this was more than just a physical obsession. The sight of him always had the power to make her draw her breath and become unpleasantly aware of the heat within her body. At night her dreams tormented her with the shape, but not the substance of his passion, but there was more to it than that. He had become inexpressibly dear to her.

'I've fallen in love with him,' she whispered to Jess.

That night she was quiet, hiding her fear with a remoteness she could not overcome. They were at another party. Ella had come back and was awash in a sea of chagrin and spite but too much in awe of Eliot to do anything about it. Tiffany was uncomfortable, aware of the stabbing glances she was getting. Aware, too, that most of the other people in the big, overheated room were watching the triangle with eyes that were avid and greedy for gossip.

Eliot, of course, coped with the situation superbly. He was never less than pleasant to Ella, but he kept Tiffany firmly tucked in beside him, smiling at her with his lazy, virile charm. And in the bright depths of his eyes there was a warning.

As he sometimes did he came in for coffee when they got home and while they were drinking it Tiffany told him that she thought they shouldn't see each other again.

He looked at her, eyes half-hidden beneath those unfairly long lashes. 'Why?'

'Because there's no need. I mean, I'm not pregnant.'

'What has that to do with anything?'

She was tired and hurting and she spoke clumsily. 'Well, that's why you've been escorting me around, isn't it?'

'No,' he returned calmly. 'I have been escorting you around, as you put it, because you are going to marry me. I want you to see what life is going to be like as my wife.'

'So that's what it was all about,' she said quietly although she could hear her heart shattering. 'Just a ploy to get me to marry you.'

'No ploy, I assure you. I've been courting you because that's your right. As neither you nor Geoffrey trusted me with the truth we started off all wrong, but there's no need for you to miss out entirely on the pleasures of being wooed.'

She looked at him, her eyes dark with secrets. 'That sounds like something from a guide to Victorian lovers. Have you been talking to your mother about me?'

So far she had not been invited to meet Mrs Buchanan, an omission which had made her wonder several times exactly what Eliot had in mind for her.

'I'm long past the age of relying on my mother for advice on how to treat women,' he returned, his irritation not quite concealing a note of surprise.

So he had discussed her with his mother. Not that he would need to do that to have his honourable *stupid* convictions reinforced. Virgins were respected and treated with care; she had been a virgin so he would do the decent thing and marry her and they could both live unhappily ever after.

No way. Marie had taken the only sensible course when she got out of Geoffrey's life. Her daughter would not be less strong.

Her resolution stiffened her spine. 'It doesn't matter,' she said in a neutral voice, carefully avoiding his eyes. 'Because I'm not going to marry you, not now, not ever. It wouldn't work.'

'Then why,' he asked silkily, 'have you been going out with me?'

Her reply needed a deep breath but if she took it he would know she was not being truthful. Her voice sounded tinny in her ears, thin with stress as she lied, 'Because I fancy you like mad. I'll be your mistress if you want me to but I won't marry you.'

Silence like the moment before an earthquake rolls the ground into destruction and death. Somehow Tiffany's hands had clasped themselves together in front of her. She stood like a woman awaiting a mortal blow, her eyes fixed on her hands, her body tensed for pain.

His fingers bit into her shoulder, flinging her around to face him. He looked as if he wanted to kill her, his eyes blazing in his face, the skin stretched taut over suddenly prominent bones.

'Say that again,' he said between his teeth. 'Look at me as you say it.'

The barely leashed violence terrified her but she could not back down now. 'You heard,' she said but her voice was inaudible and she had to repeat it.

'Say it!'

She winced as his fingers tightened on the fragile bones of her shoulder. 'I said that I will sleep with you if that's what you want but I won't marry you.'

'Then if that's what you want, that's what you'll have,' he promised and pulled her into his arms and forced her mouth to open to his in a kiss which stretched her head back so far that her neck hurt.

When it was over she stared mutely at him and he smiled a slow, cruel smile and bent his head again and bit her bottom lip, gently yet with enough force to tingle.

'You hurt,' she protested, scarcely aware of what she was saying.

His mouth moved to her throat, branding the sleek skin with kisses. Against it he said thickly, 'Wives get tenderness and respect, Tiffany. This is what's left. Do you want to change your mind?'

She knew that he was going to hurt her and enjoy it. That violence she had so often sensed beneath the self-control was lying in wait for her. Her steadfast refusal to marry him had not hurt him for he did not love her but it had struck at his pride, and for that he was going to humiliate her. But she could not go back. Whatever he did to her now would be nothing like the pain she would have to suffer as his wife.

So she said 'No,' and he laughed and said, 'So be it, then,' and let her go.

She swayed, staring at him in bewilderment. The savage anger of a moment ago had been replaced by a cool polished mask from which eyes the colour of dark sapphires gleamed.

'Up the stairs,' he said, nodding towards them.

'Now?'

He lifted his eyebrows, smiling with cold mockery. 'Now. Mistresses are usually obedient, you know. And they have to be ready when their lover is.'

It was hell walking before him up the stairs, but she did it, even lifted her chin when she turned to face him inside the bedroom.

'Take your clothes off,' he commanded softly.

She swallowed. Her fingers fumbled with the long zip fastener in the superfine wool of her crimson dress.

He watched with an impassive face, but she could see the brilliant leaping lights in his eyes and her heart trembled. He waited while she worked the zip down, big and dark and dominating, intent only on punishment. His intention made the air in the room throb with tension. It seemed to pulsate with the force of their emotions.

When she stood revealed in her petticoat he ordered harshly, 'The rest. Don't hurry. I'm in the mood to be titillated.'

Shame crawled across her skin in an icy wave. She looked up into his implacable face then pulled the petticoat over her head, her hands trembling. Unnerved by the sudden return of the dangerous man who had threatened her peace of mind while Geoffrey lived, she found herself unable to protest. Her brain shrieked outrage but her lips trembled and her voice wouldn't come.

Her bra was a skin-coloured swathe of material over pale breasts. Head bent, the damp curls clustering to hide her face, she went through the motions while her heart thumped beneath her skin. It helped not to look at him but her skin crimsoned as she removed her pants and stood before him, naked as a nymph, her hands clenched against her sides, chin lifted defiantly.

'Very nice,' he drawled. 'A little stiff, but then you're not used to being a mistress, are you? Never mind, by the time I've finished with you, you'll be well broken in. Suitable for any rider.'

The schoolboyish double meaning made her face flame. Rigid, locked in a kind of trance of horror, she waited while he touched her, his hand curving possessively around her breast, enclosing the soft weight in a cup of fingers.

'Now,' he said softly, 'undress me.'

It was a purgatory. If it hadn't been for the signs of his arousal, the hoarse breathing, the damp sheen over his skin, the slight slurring of the thick words, she would not have been able to do it. But she did. Then he smiled mirthlessly and said, 'Get into bed.'

She lay tensely, expecting a painful assault but for several moments hc lay quietly beside her without touching her, his chest rising and falling as though he fought for control. Then he turned on to his side and ran his hand the length of her body, following the gentle contours with a gentleness of his own.

'God knows why you can do this to me,' he said in a voice so hesitant that she turned her head on the pillow to look at him.

The bedside light was still on; his angular features were without expression except for a narrow, humourless smile on the cruel lips. He leaned over her and his mouth sought the pink tip of one breast, enclosing it in warmth and moisture. Tiffany groaned, her body arching spasmodically. His hand moved, found the centre of her desire and the cruel, knowledgeable fingers tormented her body into a submission as ardent as it was without volition. Her hands clenched. She began to whimper, unaware of what she was doing as she drowned in sensations too sweet to bear.

CHAPTER SEVEN

LONG hours later when he left her she lay as she was, staring at the ceiling, her exhausted brain trying to make sense of what had happened. Why did it have to be this man who could wring such a response from her, make her witless, without will? What he had done to her was beyond bearing yet she had gone up in flames for him, drawn into an inferno of rapturous passion which was as destructive as it was irresistible. What was it that chained them together so tightly that his most refined cruelty could produce this ravishment of heart and brain and body?

He had not hurt her. His cruelty was too subtle for that. Using every skill at his command he had coaxed her into a sensual daze so that all that she could experience was the touch of his hands, the burning heat of his mouth, the deep, beautiful wooing of his voice. Entranced, racked with desire, she had held him in her arms, touched him with hands that trembled and skidded over his smooth, sweat-dampened skin, following his commands with a slavish trust which made her cringe with horror now.

For he had not once lost control, not even in the moment of final ecstasy when she had sobbed out his name, her wild eyes distraught under the onslaught of so much pleasure.

He had laughed and let her sleep a little time and then, remorselessly, set about making love to her again. This time he was even more gentle, rousing her emotions until everything was lost in the silent prison he had made for her. And still he was completely in command. Afterwards he had held her until she slept, not leaving until it was almost morning.

And now she lay alone in the big bed while the tears

came, solving nothing yet not to be denied. When sleep took her again she moved uneasily, her breath catching in small sobs against the pillow.

By morning a wind came whining in from the east, redolent of league after league of stormy ocean, bitter under a bitter sky. Jess hovered reluctantly in the doorway, sniffing, her brows furrowed and her ears twitching.

'It is very good for you,' Tiffany told her firmly. 'Blows the cobwebs from between those butterfly ears. Come on, where's your Welsh stamina? This is not the spirit that carried your countrymen to victory at Cardiff Arms Park. Except when they play the All Blacks, of course.'

Perhaps spurred on by this asperison on the national rugby team of her ancestral home, Jess sneezed, snapped at a particularly hardy fly then allowed her lead to be clipped on to her collar. Tiffany shrugged into her coat. It was strange but your heart could be breaking and yet you carried on as though everything was normal, even to cracking feeble jokes with the dog.

In the park the leafless branches bent stiffly against the wind. The grass was squelchy with rain but the smells were particularly enticing. There was no need for a game of ball to encourage Jess to run. Her busy little body trekked back and forth, back and forth, nose on the alert a fraction of an inch above the ground.

Hands rammed in the pockets of her jacket Tiffany watched the dog, trying to follow her example by emptying her mind of anything but the physical reality of the moment. It was not easy, for she was afraid. In the turbulence of last night she had given the matter no consideration but the thought which had woken her that morning had been the possibility of being pregnant.

'I'll have to see a doctor,' she muttered and tried to remember the name of the sandy-haired man who had been so impersonally kind when she was sick. But he was Eliot's doctor. Better to ask Mrs Crowe the name of hers.

'Dr Fisher,' her neighbour told her. 'He's so nice, not so young that he's embarrassing and not too old to be out of date. His rooms are above the shops.' She looked at Tiffany's face, flushed with the wind and a stupid shame.

'Are you fully recovered, my dear? Should you be exercising Jess yet? I'll be happy to take her walkies, you know.'

'You've been so kind,' Tiffany told her gratefully, 'I think it's doing me the world of good to get out.'

'Yes, you are probably right,' the older woman agreed. 'But don't overdo it, will you?'

Tiffany smiled. 'No, I promise not to.'

But she had orders to catch up on and stock to make if she was going to keep her reputation for reliability, as well as her solvency. So she sewed until her head ached, drank a cup of coffee and took a painkiller and then went back to it while the wind groaned around the units. Just before midday she rang the doctor's surgery and made an appointment, wondering with hot-cheeked embarrassment if she was doing the right thing. When he left her last night Eliot had been far from forthcoming. She might never see him again, but if he accepted her offer then more lovemaking could only end in pregnancy. And that was something she could not cope with.

'Oh, God,' she whispered as she put the receiver down. She felt smirched and beaten, all her high ideals crushed by her love for a man who felt only a devouring hunger mixed with resentment for her. While she would die for him.

When the telephone began to ring she stared at it as if she was going mad before picking it up.

It was Eliot. 'Who were you ringing?' he asked curtly.

She swallowed. 'Just a shop. To tell them their order will be a little late.' Lying came hard to her but she would not—could not—tell him of her appointment with the doctor.

'Don't work too hard. You're still not completely fit yet, you know.'

No? Then why—but she knew why he had forced her into last night's exhausting lovemaking, just as she knew why she had responded so fiercely. Because neither had been able to resist the storm of passion.

'I'm going away this afternoon,' he said after a pause. 'I don't know how long I'll be gone, but it shouldn't be much more than a week. I'll be in touch when I get back.'

Desolation. Wincing with the cold of it she had to cough to clear her throat and when she did speak each word was husky. 'I see. Have a good time.'

He sounded irretrievably remote. 'I doubt it,' he said, then, 'take care of yourself, Tiffany. What would you like me to bring you back?'

The sneering note in his voice brought her head upright. 'Nothing, thank you,' she said coldly. 'Just you.'

'Oh, you'll get me,' he said, laughing softly. 'Until next week then.'

Before she had time to formulate some kind of farewell he was gone, the receiver humming emptily in her hand.

She missed him. Stupid words, for they revealed nothing of the bitter vacuum of the next few days. Work stopped her from spending every waking minute longing for him, so she worked all day and often into the night but each morning she woke with a raw feeling of incompleteness as though during the night someone had torn away half of her being.

And she dreamt of him, not the erotic fantasies which had tormented her before, but sagas of loss and loneliness and fear so that she woke shivering and crying, her whole being suffused with a need which was an agony.

Slowly she realised what she had done when she had told him that she would not marry him. She loved him and she had turned her back on that love, making it a lesser thing, reducing it to one of its components, desire. And by doing that she had lost her chance of changing his feelings for her into anything but the bitter lust which made minutes rapturous and the days bleak. And the future intolerable, both the months as his mistress and the years without him when he discarded her.

It hurt now to remember her mother's words about romance.

'It's a very good ingredient,' she had said. 'Romance adds a special lustre to a marriage. Just don't ever feel that it is the only thing necessary. There must be respect and affection and a community of interest. And always remember that in this world there are many men who will inspire all of those in you.'

Now Tiffany sighed and leaned her head on her hand. Perhaps Marie was right. Perhaps in the future there would be a man who would inspire love in her again but at the moment, when her body yearned for his and she ached for Eliot's presence, she doubted it.

'Come back,' she whispered. 'Come back, my love.'

When he did she was setting out to walk Jess. It was Saturday and he had been away ten days. As the car stopped she stopped and looked at him and her heart turned over.

He wore a casual shirt in a subdued gold and brown check, and trousers which hugged his heavily muscled thighs. The sun struck fiery sparks from his hair. He looked younger and almost carefree, a far cry from the taut lawyer she had known until then.

When Jess had been placated he straightened up and came to Tiffany who was standing frozen by the door. He was smiling but his narrowed eyes were very keen as they scanned her face.

'You look as though you've been working too hard,' he said softly and bent his head and kissed her, not gently but not hard either.

For a second she stood rigid in his grasp then her hands fastened on to his arms and she clung, pressing herself against him while stupid tears glazed her eyes.

Not that he saw them. He rested his cheek on her

hair, saying, 'I think it's time Jess saw a cow. Corgis are cattle dogs, you know. Go and get whatever you'll need for a day in the country and we'll go.'

Her voice was husky. 'Will I need to change?'

'No, you look very suitable. Have you a pair of gumboots? Good, then bring them. And whatever else you need. We'll come home after dinner.'

'Oh.'

'What is it?'

Her heart was beating heavily in her ears. She turned her head and ventured the first move she had ever made towards him, pressing her mouth against his throat. 'I'm not dressed for dinner,' she said.

'If you keep that up you won't be dressed at all.' But his cupped hand held the back of her head still and she kissed him again, touching the smooth skin with the tip of her tongue to enjoy the salt taste, every sense stretched to take in his dear presence.

'Have you missed me?' he asked thickly.

Black curls danced as she nodded and he laughed and released her, pushing her towards the door with a slap on her backside.

'Stop trying your wiles on me, you deep-eyed witch, go and get what you'll need. We'll be having dinner with my farm manager and his wife, most informally.'

So she changed her shirt for a silk one, pulled on a skirt instead of denims and wore a jersey that reflected the colour in her cheeks. And smiled at her reflection in the mirror before she straightened the bedside table, for after they arrived back tonight he would come with her up here. . . .

The day was a winter's delight, a reflection of her emotions. They drove out through the suburbs and across the harbour bridge where the man at the toll-gate wished them a good morning. The harbour sparkled beneath a brash benign sun. Although it was winter there were yachts, mostly keelers with big gull-winged sails coloured like a fleet of rainbows. Around them were the distinctive shapes of windsurfers, even gaudier of sail, their wet-suited riders enjoying the fine weather and brisk breeze.

About an hour along the enchanting route which leads north from Auckland the car turned to the right and encountered a road of such ferocious disrepair that Tiffany couldn't help a cry of shock as they hit the first enormous pot-hole.

'It has been worse,' Eliot informed her, easing the car around a vicious corner. 'The county does its best but the road really needs re-aligning and re-surfacing. And as there are only half a dozen people along it, it's not terribly high on the council's list of priorities.'

'So I see.'

He laughed but she was glad that he didn't take his eyes from the narrow, winding track ahead. Although she was not a nervous passenger, when the ground abruptly fell away on her side of the road she realised that there was no one else with whom she would feel as confident on such a stretch of road.

'How far down it do we go?'

'Until the end. Eight kilometres. It gets worse.'

It did, but Tiffany sat back, perfectly safe in such competent hands, and gazed around her with interest. Until then she had not realised how circumscribed her life had become, revolving around the house. It was good to be out in the country again, to watch the swift cloud shadows over the hills, to admire big lumbering Hereford cattle and several different sorts of sheep, including a small flock of black and dark brown ones.

Towards the end of the road the grass and neat wire fences gave way to tea-tree scrub, dusted now with small white flowers. In the hollows were patches of swampy ground, unkempt, vaguely sinister. 'This is my place,' Eliot told her.

'Have you had it long?'

'About three years. When I bought it it was all like this. We've done a lot of development but there's still a long way to go yet.'

Something in his voice made her turn her head. He

was smiling and she said on a note of wonder, 'This is what you like doing, isn't it?'

'Yes.'

The monosyllable was clipped but something emboldened her to ask, 'Better than being a lawyer?'

For a moment it seemed that he was going to ignore her but he must have been considering her question for he said thoughtfully, 'Yes, I think I do. Don't get me wrong, though. I enjoy my work very much. But this, to make the earth flourish, is something else. Not that I'm a farmer. Dick Howard does that job. I provide the money and the enthusiasm. Slightly misplaced, possibly, the way our export situation is at the moment, but we'll survive.'

Tiffany nodded. This was something she had heard often enough in her stepfather's house, and always there had been that corollary, spoken or inferred. 'We'll survive,' the age-old confidence of the land. People die, crowns disappear, governments fall, but through it all the land survives.

'Ah, here we are.' The car swung around the side of a hill and there was a house on the edge of a valley, green and secluded and silent, beneath the sun. Actually there were three houses, two neat modern bungalows set a little distance apart in their own gardens and at the other end of the valley a big old double-storeyed building huddled in a thick square of enormous macrocarpa trees.

'The original homestead,' Eliot told her laconically. 'It's in rather bad shape although I had enough repairs done to stop it from deteriorating further.'

'It looks lovely.'

'It's a pleasant place. Those trees will have to come down, of course. They're old and were planted far too close. I've put in shelter further away and when it's tall enough I'll fell those old relics.'

'Good,' she nodded. 'I hate macrocarpas—they're so gloomy. The house must be terribly dark inside.'

'It is. They were planted by someone with a

shattering lack of imagination. Or,' as the car rattled over a cattle-grid, 'absolutely no idea of how big they were going to grow.'

For some reason this struck Tiffany as amusing. She chuckled and his hand dropped briefly over hers in her lap and squeezed them together. 'We have the same sense of humour,' he said as though it was a surprise. 'I like your laugh. I don't hear it enough.'

Well no. But then he didn't exactly invite it. Wisely deciding to follow his lead and so give herself one carefree day in his company, she said nothing.

Someone was already waiting by the gate, a small, spare man, bandy-legged, with a beaming smile and a pair of shrewd grey eyes which took in every aspect of Tiffany's appearance in one lightning-swift but not unkind glance.

'This is Dick Howard,' Eliot said. 'Dick, I told you I'd be bringing Tiffany Brandon.'

'The wife's looking forward to meeting you,' Dick responded, shaking hands firmly before leading the way up a concrete path between borders of spring bulbs, clumps of jonquils and daffodils, the rigid red and gold spikes of lachenalias, silken-skirted Iceland poppies and an enormous daphne bush which scented the air with its spicy, evocative perfume.

His wife was a big woman with the most beautiful green eyes that Tiffany had ever seen in an intelligent, plain face. Her smile and welcome were more cautious though she greeted Eliot with obvious affection and respect.

She made tea for them and they spent a pleasant twenty minutes drinking it out on a terrace, bordered with daisies in pink and white and yellow, which overlooked the rolling green hills of Eliot's farm. Tiffany began to relax. Her eyes lost their bruised look as she laughed at the antics of a tiny bantam rooster which seemed to think it was human. She did not realise that Eliot's eyes seldom strayed from her or that the Howards watched them both while chatting quietly about the farm and its concerns.

Although it was the depths of winter the sun was hot, beating down through the bare stems of vine which in summer would shade the terrace. In this sheltered valley there was no wind, although above in the clear sky birds swayed on unseen air currents.

During a lull in the conversation Tiffany asked, 'Is the sea not far from here? Those are gulls, aren't they?'

'She's from the South Island,' Eliot told their hosts, smiling. 'Her geography is still shaky. The sea is about two miles over the hills. It's one of our boundaries.'

'Oh, cliffs? Or are there beaches?'

'One beach, a rather nice one although it's a bit exposed in an easterly. The rest is cliffs. Not too high, and many of them overgrown with pohutukawa trees; we have planted pines around them to break the winds from the sea.'

The sun glinted blue in Tiffany's hair when she nodded, gilded the tender curve of her mouth as she said, 'I'm looking forward to my first Christmas up here. My mother has never tired of telling us how beautiful Auckland is with the pohutukawa trees flowering in crimson and scarlet around the coast.'

'When Christmas comes we'll make a special trip up to see them,' Eliot told her blandly as he got to his feet. Before she had time to register more than astonishment he caught her by the hand. 'Come on, we'll take a tour around the place.'

'No,' she said as she was drawn inexorably to her feet. 'Wait, I'll help Mrs Howard with the dishes before we go.'

'Not at all,' the older woman insisted firmly. 'There are only a few.'

Tiffany held back but Mrs Howard smiled and finished, 'Eliot has provided us with a dishwasher, so it's no bother. Off you go now, before your dog gets sick of being tied up.'

They all laughed for Jess had been quivering with anticipation ever since they had sat down, her nose wrinkling as she tasted each new scent on the air, restrained only by Eliot's stern injunctions from leaping at the little rooster. On the way up she had slept on the back seat but this paradise of scents and sounds had her shiveringly awake.

They went in a Land Rover over an excellent system of farm tracks. Dick Howard and Eliot did most of the talking but occasionally Tiffany asked a question or ventured a comment.

'Grew up on a farm, did you?' Dick asked after one such.

She nodded. 'Yes, in the South Island. My father has a dairy herd.'

'Ah well, it's all much the same, wherever you are.' His beaming smile lit his face. 'Now Eliot here has some funny ideas about farming but they seem to work.'

'I don't like exploitation,' Eliot said in answer to Tiffany's enquiring glance. 'What is taken from the soil has to go back into it.'

He began to talk above her head to Dick about a water reticulation system, speaking tersely. Clearly he knew exactly what he was discussing. Tiffany didn't, and felt free to let her concentration waver.

A foolish thing to do, for while she had been thinking of the farm she could almost manage to ignore the man who sat beside her. Now that part of her which was so closely attuned to him was free to waken and expand so that she was suddenly, acutely aware of the hard tensile strength of the thigh which pressed against hers, the powerful shoulder and arm along the seat behind her. The track was well-made but roughly metalled; when the Land Rover negotiated some pot-holes she was jolted against him. Instantly his arm curved around her shoulder, holding her steady. Now she was self-consciously tense, especially when his hand slid beneath her arm to rest against her breast.

Not by the movement of a single muscle did Dick Howard reveal that he realised what had happened but Tiffany could feel his alert interest as if he had beamed it at them like a lighthouse.

Heat prickled up her neck and across her cheekbones. 'How's Jess getting on in the back?' she asked, almost croaking the words.

Eliot tightened his hold to prevent her from turning. 'Fine,' he said briefly and went on with his conversation with Dick, the words flowing smoothly over Tiffany's head.

Seething with anger and the potent hunger he induced in her, she listened, her gaze directed rigidly ahead. His touch was a taunt, an underlining of his lack of respect. 'Wives get respect,' he had said. Now he was making abundantly clear what she had forfeited by her refusal to marry him.

Yet even as she felt the familiar wash of humiliation she was conscious of another, deeper emotion. And it was shaming too, this shuddering anticipation which sharpened her senses so that she could smell his faint masculine scent, see from the corner of her eye his profile, arrogant and angular against the pure blue of the sky. Unbidden to her mouth came the salty taste of him. Her fingers curled impotently in her lap as they remembered exactly how his skin flowed smooth like warm silk over muscle and sinew and bone.

He was like an aphrodisiac to her, a love potion incomparably stronger than will-power or principles or strength of mind. In his presence she was another Tiffany Brandon, ageless, spellbound and helpless against the dark power of his masculinity. He had only to meet her eyes or smile at her and she waited in abject surrender, waited to be taken.

And although she was shamed by her weakness she gloried in it, too, for her weakness was her strength. The tension which sparked between them was not just one way; he, too, waited for her touch, and when it came his surrender was as complete. Except that last time he had managed to retain his self-control. Not so much that he could walk away from her, but enough to give his loving that impersonal, almost mechanical quality which had made her cry when he left her. He had punished her because she would not surrender her independence, and she knew with an instinct which still surprised her that he punished her because he wanted her with a desperation he feared and despised.

Yet he could not reject her. Whatever he felt for her was strong enough to bind him to her. For all of his glittering sophistication, his experience and the power he wielded, he was hers as much as she was his.

She turned her head a little, tilting it so that she could see into his face. He ignored the slight movement even though her curls brushed his throat. His eyes were fixed on Dick Howard; Tiffany watched the firm, chiselled mouth move, listened to his deep, beautiful voice without hearing the words he spoke. And after a time—minutes, hours?—his lashes drooped and his gaze was captured. For long moments they stared at each other, both faces set in an almost identical expression. His mouth thinned and something glittered deep in his eyes, summoning up the small golden lights in hers, dancing, weaving patterns as the Land Rover swayed around the side of a hill and she stared at him in astonishment and comprehension.

Beneath the tan his skin gained colour as a tiny nerve began to flick close to his mouth. Tiffany couldn't breathe. Her heart leapt into her throat, blocking it so that she had to swallow hard.

Then Dick Howard said something in his pleasant voice and shattered the spell. Against her breast Eliot's hand clenched, the knuckles pressing hard into the soft curve before it lifted away to come to rest again along the back of the seat. He replied, his expression remote, shuttered against all emotion. Tiffany swallowed again and turned her head away from him, watching Dick's thick, capable hands on the wheel.

At the top of the hill the vehicle slowed to a halt.

'Good view from here,' Dick said cheerfully, apparently unmoved by the tension in the cab.

Eliot got out and swung round to let Jess out of the back, leaving Tiffany to get down without help. Not that she needed it but he was so punctilious that the absence of his normal effortless courtesy was an indication of his stress.

'How good is she at coming when she's called?' he asked.

Tiffany shrugged, smiling at Jess who was pulling hard on the leash. 'In the park she's perfect. Whether she'll be quite as good here, I don't know.'

'We'll try her.'

As soon as the leash had been slipped Jess tore off across the short grass, head down, ears pricked alertly. But when Tiffany called her she returned immediately although she looked a little quizzical.

'OK, good girl,' Tiffany said. 'Off you go now.'

Dick had chosen his vantage point well. Almost the highest point on the farm, it gave a superb view over the lush green pastures near the homestead to the dull grey-green hills which still had to be brought in. And beyond the sombre green of pine plantations was a slice of the sea, vividly blue against the carbon paper outline of a high mountainous stretch of land on the horizon.

'Oh,' she breathed. 'It is lovely.'

Dick was pleased by the rapt expression on her face. 'That's Coromandel,' he said pointing. 'And that lower bit north of it is Great Barrier Island. That tiny dot between them is Cuvier Island.'

Summoning up her mental map of the North Island Tiffany nodded. 'Yes, I've placed them,' she said, adding, 'somehow I didn't expect to see mountains. Apart from the central volcanoes and Egmont, I've never imagined mountains in the North Island.'

'Oh, you South Islanders think you have a monopoly on them,' Eliot teased lightly. 'Moehu, on Coromandel, is almost three thousand feet high.'

She laughed, met his cold gaze with equanimity. 'Well, but that's only a *hill*! Where I come from, a mountain is a mountain! Twelve thousand feet or so.'

'You live on top of Mount Cook?' he asked, naming New Zealand's highest mountain.

She gave a light answer and turned away, shaken by the contrast between his teasing voice and the total lack of warmth in his eyes. She began to ask questions about the farm, drawing the farm manager into the conversation; he was eager enough, pointing out various areas of interest, telling anecdotes in some of which Eliot figured prominently.

'Don't take any notice of him,' Eliot interrupted one particularly glowing effort. 'It was nothing, just a drive into town.'

'After you'd splinted the chap's leg and taken the Rover up a hill no sane man would have tackled,' Dick said obstinately. 'No nerves, that's your trouble. Look, there's the hill, that one with the gully and the clump of taraire trees half-way up. Eliot saw the bulldozer go over and came belting along to the house, shouted at the wife, then he shot off in the Rover as if it was judgment day. By the time I got there he'd managed to get the 'dozer driver splinted up and into the 'Rover and was on his way back. I got in the back with the kid and held his hand. Scared the—scared the hell out of me, I can tell you. I doubt if the kid would have taken his bulldozer down some of the hills we went down. Eliot got the Rover back to the house in no time flat and we met the doctor there. He reckoned that it was the speed which helped save the driver's leg. Halved the chance of infection.'

Tiffany had been staring at the hill he indicated with appalled eyes. It was green and smooth and to her it looked almost vertical. Even a bulldozer would have difficulty staying upright on it, she thought and shivered.

'Foolhardy,' she said, switching her gaze to Eliot's face. 'Don't you do anything like that again.'

The cold penetrating eyes scrutinised her face. 'Ah, but I didn't know you then,' he said hatefully.

Tiffany flinched as he threaded a finger through her curls and tugged gently. On the edge of her vision she could see Dick's beaming face and knew exactly what he was thinking. It probably wouldn't occur to him that Eliot wasn't referring to a love which would have its inevitable fulfilment in marriage. But Eliot knew, and was deliberately taunting her with her decision.

For a moment she felt an overwhelming desire for her mother. Only for a moment, for this was a situation she had to fight through by herself. Marie's calm common sense was no help to her now. This war she and Eliot fought was private, just between the two of them. There was no place in it for anyone else. Not Marie, not Dick.

'Well, don't do anything like that again,' she said, smiling as though she was teasing.

Dick chuckled against the quiet singing of the wind and the clear call of a skylark. Tiffany's eyes slid from their perusal of Eliot's face to that terrifyingly steep hill and an image flashed into her mind of him, broken and bleeding, his splendid body twisted in pain. A stark fear caught her by the throat and she looked back at him, her pupils wide, to reassure herself. Beads of sweat sprang across her forehead.

'What is it?' he asked sharply. 'What's the matter?'

'A goose walked over my grave.'

He didn't believe her but he said nothing, just put his arm around her as she shivered and hugged her close against his warm strength.

'Do you want to go back to the homestead?'

'No,' she said, recovering herself. 'No, of course not.'

She managed to push the image to the back of her mind and set herself out to be interested. Not that it took very much effort. She admired the woodlots which had been planted, some of Eliot's 'notions', she gathered from Dick's reference to them. Certainly they were different, carob and honey locust trees for stock food, a stand of black walnut, small yet, but in a hundred years' time they would have matured enough to be immensely valuable. The gullies had been left to regenerate into native bush and were carefully fenced off so that stock couldn't crush the new growth.

'There are lots more trees than usual, aren't there?'

she asked, looking at a little cluster of totara which had been enclosed at the top of a hill.

Eliot nodded. 'I have this theory that both stock and grass do better for a little shelter,' he told her. 'Dick doesn't believe it, but he puts up with my strange ideas.'

Dick grinned. 'Well, every man's entitled to a hobby horse,' he said laconically. 'When he's prepared to put up the money for it, more so.'

There were dams scooped out by the bulldozer which had tried to kill its driver, surrounded by more trees, both natives and, on the edge, crab-apples and berry bushes to attract birds. In a clump of taraire trees in one of the valleys they watched in absorbed silence as two big, lazy native pigeons sat in quiet harmony on a branch, plump white breasts gleamingly contrasted with bronze-green plumage.

'They're such stupid birds,' Dick said softly. 'They'll sit there and let you knock them down. Illegal, of course.'

'Oh, but they're so lovely.' Tiffany watched, her face entranced.

It was a perfect moment, a perfect day of blue and green and the white of the cloud castles, the high-pitched singing of invisible skylarks, the gentle calling of ewes to their new-born lambs. In spite of the sun's warmth the air was cool but the wind had dropped and the very briskness added to the day's delights. Jess frolicked like a small, busy tank over the grass, only having to be reprimanded once when her ancestral instincts came to the fore and she headed for a group of flighty young Herefords.

'Well, she is a cattle dog,' Tiffany pointed out when Eliot's incisive command had brought the dog back with quite obvious reluctance.

'Not my cattle.' But Eliot bent and stroked the sharp little head with an affectionate hand.

A paradox: cruel and kind, harsh and gentle, honourable and ruthless. A complex, sophisticated man who wanted her in spite of himself. The man she loved in spite of herself. Tiffany smiled down at the two of them, dog and man, small foxy head against the glowing mahogany highlights of Eliot's hair, the pure, austere lines of his face and head and neck, strong and unbearably beautiful to her.

He stood up and caught her eyes, held them in a long, mocking stare and then with a sardonic twist to his lips took her hand and urged her back towards the Land Rover.

'Dick can't exist more than two and a half hours without a cup of tea,' he said.

Back at the house, Mrs Howard had obviously been waiting for them and, sure enough, the table was set for an elaborate afternoon tea which they all, including Jess who was surreptitiously fed by Mrs Howard, enjoyed.

CHAPTER EIGHT

'Too much,' Tiffany sighed as they made their way across the short green turf to the old homestead behind its screen of conifers. 'Isn't she a marvellous cook!'

'Extremely good.' He spoke abruptly, his expression shuttered.

Tiffany stole a look at him before turning away. As always, excitement pulled hard through her body, ached deep in her bones, and she thought of her bed at home. Unbidden colour flaked across her cheekbones as the serenity of her dark eyes was disturbed.

Deliberately she began to breathe with even care, concentrating on the reduction of the tide of desire which flowed hotly to meet him.

'How old is the homestead?' she asked.

'Dick was told that it was built a hundred years ago. If it was, it escaped the Victorian mania for fuss and frills. As you'll see, it has a faintly Georgian air.'

It had, too, evoked by the wide verandas and colonnade only two steps above the lawn. Overshadowed by big old trees it was gloomy and cold but, as they walked through the large, high-ceilinged rooms, Tiffany could imagine how attractive it could be.

'It needs a lot done to it,' she said, looking with appalled eyes at the horror that was the kitchen.

Eliot smiled. 'It does, indeed. When I first saw it the walls billowed whenever the wind blew. It is all scrimmed, of course. What would you do to it?'

She was tempted, but something in his smile made her shake her head. 'You'd need a professional to realise its full potential.'

'Do you think so?' The words were drawled with an unpleasant undertone which warned her that her instinct had been right. 'You made an excellent job of the town house.'

'Compared with this the town house is child's play.'

'I thought all women liked the chance to spend an enormous amount of money on their home.'

She flinched, but he moved faster than she, catching her by the shoulders to pull her close against his tense body.

'I thought that when we have children we could move here,' he said, clearly, daring her to object. 'The road is appalling, I know, but we can do something about that. And there is a school not very far away. It would be a good place to bring up children.'

She stood very rigid, not giving way at all. 'I'm sure it would be,' she said. 'But we are not having children, Eliot.'

'Don't you want children?'

Very pale, very defiant, she stared up into his remorseless face. 'Not yours.'

'A pity.' His mouth hardened, then was lowered to rest lightly on hers. 'Of course, if the idea of having children frightens you then we'll not have them. My mother will be disappointed, but it's our life, not hers.'

He knew—he must know—how he was hurting. Through lips which were pale and stiff she said woodenly, 'I'm not going to marry you, Eliot.'

He laughed, his breath warm like a little caress on her mouth. 'Of course you are,' he said. 'Where do you think I've spent the last few days?'

'Where?' she whispered.

'Getting to know your family.'

He watched with cold amusement as she put out a hand in protest, her face dead white, her eyes huge as they held his imploringly.

'No,' she said beneath her breath. 'No, Eliot.'

'Yes, Tiffany.' The words mocked but there was wry approval in his voice as he continued, 'We got on very well together. I think your stepfather was rather touched that I came to ask him for your hand. I didn't, of course, tell him that I'd already bedded his step-daughter. I have the feeling he might have found that hard to forgive. But I'm sure even he would agree that I was doing the right thing by marrying you.'

'How could you?' The words broke from her as she lifted a hand to slap the cynical amusement from the face. 'I could kill you,' she said as her hand connected.

It hurt, but she enjoyed the pain, watched with bitter, angry eyes as the dark skin paled and then reddened with the force of her blow.

Eliot smiled mirthlessly but said nothing, his lids lowered so that all she could see of his eyes was a brilliant sliver of colour.

'I'm not going to marry you,' she said and said it again, more harshly. 'Never. Not even if my entire family have fallen for that specious charm you use like a weapon. Can't you get it into your head? I do not *want* to marry you! I can think of nothing worse than to be shackled to you until you get sick of whatever it is that you want of me and divorce me. I'd rather die!'

'Than be divorced?' He spoke through his teeth, his hands tightening on her slim shoulders with cruel force. 'You needn't ever concern yourself about divorce. I don't believe in it. Besides, what I feel for you is not going to be assuaged by a few years' access to your body, my dear. I suppose it's your charming lack of experience which makes it difficult for you to understand that I want you. All of you. I want to own you, Tiffany, body and heart and soul. I want to know that when you look at me you'll know your master.'

Appalled, she thought his hands were going to crush the bones in her shoulders. She began to shake her head, afraid as she had never been before, for she saw something in his expression, heard a note in his voice which terrified her with its dark purpose.

'You can't,' she said helplessly. 'I won't let you.'

'You can't stop me.'

He let her go and walked across to the window, a dark silhouette against the deep green of the encroaching trees. For a long moment he stared out then turned only his head, not looking at her so that all that she could see of him was his face in profile, as beautiful and emotionless as that on a coin.

When he spoke his voice was cold, almost casually light. 'If you don't marry me,' he said calmly, 'I'll tell your stepfather the exact circumstances of your conception. A religious man, your stepfather, isn't he? Almost rigid in his views. He has a hatred of lies and deceit.'

Tiffany flinched then put her hands up to her face. She had thought that he had hurt her so much that she could never be hurt again, but he was diabolically clever at discovering new ways to cause pain.

It was at that moment that she gave up. She knew—none better—that George found it hard to forgive those who lied to him. Basically a kind man, he fought what he saw as a sin, but if he discovered that his wife had deceived him, and gone on deceiving him, it would ruin their marriage. Marie had known this when she asked Geoffrey not to reveal his relationship to Tiffany. If Eliot carried out his threat then Marie would lose so much—and so would her husband.

The sound of Tiffany's breath sobbed through the dark, still room.

'Well?' Eliot sounded tired but the note of determination was inflexible.

He would destroy the world just so that he could have the pleasure of dragging her down into the ruins with him.

'Why?' she asked pitifully.

The broad shoulders lifted in a shrug. 'God knows. Do you think I want it to be this way? If I could I'd take what you so generously offer, sate myself in your delectable little body and walk away laughing as soon as you bored me. But I can't. Perhaps you appeal to the chauvinist in me.'

'Will it be worth it? Marriage to a woman who hates you just for the pleasure of taking her to bed?'

He laughed and moved at last, coming back to pick up her hand and lift it to his mouth. 'But I don't want just the pleasure of having you in my bed,' he said, and bit the mound beneath her thumb, quite gently.

Tiffany's fingers curled at the erotic caress. The sensation of his teeth and tongue on her skin sent a lick of fire through her veins.

'That's called the mound of Venus,' he said, watching her, his expression sardonic. 'You can see why, can't you? No, I don't want just your sexual services, Tiffany. I want you.'

The words sounded with flat emphasis. Shivering, Tiffany expelled a sighing breath.

'Very well,' she said dully, resigning herself to a lifetime of subtle humiliation and pain. Not that he would always be deliberately cruel. He could be an enchanting companion. She might even be happy. But always, like a canker in her life, there would be the knowledge that he did not love her. Whatever he felt for her was so strong that it overbore his immense will-power, but it was not love.

'Shall we seal it in the time-honoured fashion?' he asked gravely, almost as though he understood her weary despair.

The kiss was gentle but she could not relax for she was too aware of the restraint he was keeping on himself. After a moment he muttered, 'Oh, what's the use . . .' and brought his mouth down hard on hers, forcing it to open beneath lips and a tongue as cruel as death.

Everything that was kind and laughing and loving might have died in her but what was left, the merciless enchantment, spread in a wave of fire throughout her body so that she clung, pressing herself against the hard impatience of his body, her eyes closed against the triumph she knew she would see in his face.

Deep in his throat he groaned and lifted his head a fraction so that he could press hard, open-mouthed kisses against her throat and within the neckline of her shirt. Mindless pleasure made her shudder; her hands gripped his back, feeling the tension of the muscles as he stooped. When he began to free the buttons of her shirt she made no protest, the dark depths of her eyes blind to everything but the sight of him.

Beneath his hand her breasts bloomed. He watched as his fingers caressed them, the lean strength dark against her pale skin. She shivered again, her skin tightening.

'So beautiful,' he said thickly. 'You are so beautiful. I wish . . .'

She moaned as she pulled his head down, lost now in the familiar sensations. This was what she had been waiting for ever since the last time, this warm, golden sea of feeling which blotted out all thought, all principles and standards, left her with nothing to do but to surrender to the excitement of his mouth on her skin, secure in the knowledge that soon that would not be enough for either of them.

And when that happened, when she was racked with the intensity of her hunger, then he would ease it in the only way possible, with the deep thrusting drive of his body.

After that there would be the familiar, grinning companions, shame and guilt and anger, but first there would come the ecstasy and fulfilment and the lazy lassitude of satisfaction.

When he lifted his head she whimpered, curling a hand around his face in an attempt to keep it against her. Beneath her fingers his skin was hot and dry as if he had a fever; his jaw was rigid.

'Not here,' he said harshly. 'Not now, Tiffany.'

'Yes,' she whispered, kissing him as he had taught her to, her tongue tasting the salty, masculine tang of him. 'Please, Eliot, yes.'

'Here? Do you want me to take you here?' His voice cracked the intense sexual aura surrounding them like a whip going through fragile glass. He shook her, saying grimly, 'Shall I take you here on the floor, Tiffany, tumble you on the bare boards?'

Her dilated eyes were fixed on to his face. She thought she could read there contempt and anger and her hands came up to cover her face so that she could hide behind them.

'No,' he muttered, dragging them down so that she was exposed to him. He was as pale as he had been flushed; the blazing passion had faded leaving a fleeting anguish and then blankness. More gently he said, 'Not here, my darling, although I want you desperately. I can wait. Don't look like that, please, Tiffany.'

'How do I look?' she asked bitterly. 'Shamed? Well, I feel ashamed.'

Grabbing the lapels of her shirt she forced the buttons into their holes, bringing all of her concentration to bear on the small task to give herself time to fight free from the frustration which was stinging along her nerves and through her blood, making her raw with hunger and need. He moved away, tucking in the shirt which had somehow come free from his trousers.

No, not *somehow*, she thought with savage disgust. She had pulled it free so that she could slide her hands over his back. He would have felt the sensual movement of her fingers, the sheer tactile delight with which she had stroked and touched him, delighting in the smooth, strong warmth of his body. And when his mouth had closed on to her breast he must have felt her hands clench in a blind pleasure so intense that she could still feel it beating through her veins.

Disgust at her wanton response to his soulless desire was written on her features as she turned towards the door. She looked small and beaten, her shoulders sagging. It was her spiritual nadir, the moment when she realised that she was bound to him by the most powerful chains in the world.

'Tiffany,' he said quietly.

She stopped, unable to look at him. His forefinger tilted her chin; for a long moment he scrutinised her face. Then he said 'It doesn't matter,' and took her elbow in an oddly impersonal grip.

It was quite late when they got home. They had had a pleasant evening with the Howards and then driven home through a clear night. And in spite of herself Tiffany could not prevent the quickening of her heartbeats as they approached Auckland. But although he came in with her and checked the house out he did no more than kiss her on the forehead before he left.

There followed a dreamlike time. The next evening they dined with Eliot's mother, who had all Eliot's charm and only a little of his toughness and who made it quite clear that she welcomed Tiffany with relief. 'It is,' she said gaily, 'time I had some grandchildren.'

After dinner Eliot put a call through to the South Island and told a happy Marie that he had succeeded in persuading their daughter to marry him.

He did it beautifully, one arm around Tiffany, his voice proud and happy, with never a hint of blackmail or the darker emotions which lay beneath the elegant, sophisticated surface.

'We're so thrilled for you, love,' Marie told Tiffany excitedly. 'We like him so much. The boys are suffering from an exaggerated case of hero-worship.'

Her voice invited Tiffany to share the joke. Held in Eliot's arm, his heart beating strongly against her cheek, Tiffany smiled and chattered and managed to imitate the Tiffany Brandon her mother had known.

'I don't suppose you'll be having the wedding here,' Marie said wistfully.

'I—I hadn't thought.' Tiffany's whole being rebelled at going through with this empty charade under the loving eyes of her family but before she could say anything Eliot took the receiver, saying that of course they would be married from Tiffany's home; only a small wedding as he had few relatives. The deep resonant voice soothed and encouraged and when Tiffany had recovered her composure the receiver was handed back and she was able to talk to her stepfather and her two half-brothers, respond as best she could to his quiet good wishes and their diffident teasing, and then it was over.

And she was crying, great sobs from nowhere, embarrassing tears, wretchedness so profound that she thought she might die from it.

Eliot's arms held her, it was his handkerchief she used to try to stem the worst of the flow, but it was Mrs Buchanan who said, 'Poor child, I suppose you're overwrought and missing your family like mad. Eliot, stop clutching her as though she's going to disappear. Go and get some brandy.'

'Not brandy,' Eliot said in response to Tiffany's convulsive shudder. 'She doesn't like the stuff.'

'Liking has nothing to do with it,' his mother told him firmly. 'Start as you mean to go on, Eliot. She needs *something*.'

The strong male arms were replaced by a female one. Tiffany gulped and blew her nose and dabbed at the tears which dripped forlornly, then allowed herself to be led to a sofa.

'Too much excitement,' Mrs Buchanan pronounced, sounding so like Marie that Tiffany got caught between a chuckle and a sob and had to be patted on the back until the coughing stopped.

By then Eliot was back with a glass containing a suspicious looking liquid. 'Whisky,' he told her. 'And drain the lot.'

It was horrible but it did stop the tears and after a few minutes had a pleasantly relaxing effect on her. So much so that after her first two yawns Mrs Buchanan suggested she stay the night.

'Oh, no thank you. I've left Jess shut in the house,' Tiffany explained quickly.

'Well, of course you must go home then.' Mrs Buchanan smiled at her with what seemed to be real affection before switching her attention to her son. 'Don't keep her up too late, Eliot. She needs her sleep. The poor child looks smudged around the eyes.'

'Too much excitement,' he mocked blandly, but his glance was bleak as it rested on Tiffany's face.

Once more he checked the house before saying

good night but this time his kiss was the kind she
dreaded; his mouth took hers in a frenzy of desire as
though he felt an angry need to impress his strength on
her. And she was powerless against her answering
passion. She wanted to give him what he craved for, her
complete surrender, and knew that she dared not. If
once he realised that she loved him he would have the
ultimate weapon. One that he would use in this silent
battle they fought.

'Sleep well,' he said huskily, his mouth hot against
her eyelids. Slowly his hands moved the length of her
back, holding her against him so that she felt his
arousal.

'I'd kill for this,' he breathed raggedly. 'Do you want
me, Tiffany?'

She shivered, refusing to answer and he laughed and
said, 'You're a coward, my darling. One day you'll
admit just how much you want me, again and again
until I tire of hearing it.'

Another searing kiss and he was gone, leaving her to
hold back the sobs with one hand pressed to her mouth.

The days followed each other in a kind of haze. All
decisions were made by Eliot. He decreed that they
should marry in a month's time and that Tiffany was to
fly down a week before the wedding. Fortunately she
was ahead on her orders but she found herself using her
work as a crutch, sewing every spare minute that she
had between choosing a wedding dress and a trousseau
under Mrs Buchanan's benign and discerning eye.

At first Tiffany had objected to the amount of money
represented by the wardrobe Mrs Buchanan thought
necessary, only to be kindly reprimanded.

'Although Eliot is a very private person he leads quite
a social life,' Mrs Buchanan said firmly. 'You must be
prepared for everything from morning teas to balls.'

'Morning teas?' Tiffany couldn't hide her horror.

A mischievous gurgle of laughter made her relax.
'Well, perhaps not,' Mrs Buchanan conceded. 'But
please don't be stuffy about clothes, my dear. You have

a very pretty little figure and it will give Eliot great pleasure to dress it—as well as undress it. He'll want to be proud of you, just as you are proud of him.' She hesitated before finishing with cool deliberation, 'I'm sure I don't have to tell you that Eliot has been considered quite a catch. Even after he's married there will be plenty of unethical young women around trying to catch his eye.'

The not too subtle warning made Tiffany smile. If this was a normal marriage she might be concerned about those predatory women, but at the moment they were the least of her worries.

'As it is,' Mrs Buchanan said, her alert eyes missing nothing, 'you'll be faced with several of them tomorrow night. I couldn't leave them out as we have known them since they were children and their parents forever.'

Tomorrow night was the engagement party. It had started out to be a small affair but Mrs Buchanan professed to be unable to limit the numbers and Eliot had given in. Tiffany should have been terrified at the thought of meeting so many friends and relations but the cocoon she inhabited insulated her from such fears. She had chosen her dress, a pretty silk thing the gold of the flecks in her eyes, and was resigned to being on show. Not even the certainty of meeting some of Eliot's past girlfriends could shake the strange lethargy of her emotions.

Which was just as well, for almost the first person to arrive at the Buchanans' big old house that night was Ella Sheridan, the woman Eliot had been escorting the night Geoffrey took her to Flamingo's! And, after smiling with the bare minimum of courtesy at Tiffany, Ella drew Eliot's head down and kissed him enthusiastically on the mouth.

'Darling, you look—tired,' she drawled, slanting a quick glance at Tiffany to see how she reacted. 'Or worried. Things harassing you?'

He grinned down into her beautiful face. 'Neither, Ella. Now, behave yourself, or Tiffany will think you have no manners.'

'Well, I never did let concern for good manners get in my way,' she returned provocatively before taking herself off, hips swaying with seductive emphasis beneath the scarlet material of her dress. She had certainly dressed for show in a one-shouldered dress of vaguely Spanish design, slinky and sinuous until it broke into a froth of frills at thigh level.

'At least pretend to look jealous,' Eliot murmured into Tiffany's ear. 'She's watching us out of the corner of her eyes.'

'Well, she certainly tried hard enough.' Tiffany's eyes strayed beyond the firm outline of his lips, met the cool sardonic blue of his gaze. 'Would you like me to cling to your arm and glower at any woman under forty who comes within ten feet of you?' She smiled. 'Sorry,' she said lightly.

'Liar. You don't care about Ella's histrionics because you know that I couldn't care less about her—or any other woman'.

She noticed that his breathing was uneven—pacing hers. They stood facing each other, lost for a moment in the all-encompassing circle of their mutual need, absorbed face bent to absorbed face, held fast in a kind of spell.

Until Mrs Buchanan, elegant in lilac, interrupted the silent communication. And then Geoffrey's daughter, Diana March, and her husband arrived, he looking wary, she with a discontented expression to mar her pretty face.

She was sullenly effusive, determined to gloss over the awkwardness. Yet as they smiled and pretended, they were all aware of the concealed interest of those other guests, all of whom knew that before his death Geoffrey Upcott had been seen in Tiffany's company.

But Diana was on her best behaviour, as was Colin, her brother, when he arrived a little later and Eliot with his urbane self-assurance made the whole situation seem almost normal.

What liars we all are, Tiffany thought, hours later.

All hidden behind our masks, revealing ourselves by omission, by tiny slips made in moments of forgetfulness and stress.

She stared at her hand, slender on Eliot's shoulder as they danced, the diamond he had chosen for her engagement ring glittering on her finger. Against the dark cloth of his sleeve her hand looked pale and fragile; she could feel the warmth of his body through the material. In a way he was her protector, keeping Ella and Diana and all the others at bay, yet he was the one who had blackmailed her into being here. Dominant, powerful, but helpless in the grip of a hunger which went far beyond the bounds of normality.

Once she had dreamed of a love kind and gentle and considerate. What she had been granted was not love, nor was it kind and gentle, yet he had only to look at her and she trembled with need and desire.

And a deep, wrenching pain, for what she felt was love and although he wanted her he did not love her. If he had he would not have used her love for her mother to force her into this situation.

'You're very silent.' he commented quietly. 'Our guests will be thinking that we have just had our first quarrel.'

'Then they will be wrong.' Of course they were being covertly watched.

'Do you think so?' He answered smoothly the lift of her brows. 'We have never actually quarrelled, I feel. All our—altercations—have been rather like prize fights, knock-down affairs with victory rarely conceded.'

'Well, you've won,' she said, faint bitterness colouring her voice.

'Have I? No, I've lost. The ultimate victory is yours.'

She stared up at him, meeting the cold irony of his expression with puzzlement in her eyes. 'Hardly. You have what you've wanted.'

'I have your resentful and reluctant acquiescence,' he returned coolly.

She understood and colour came and went in her face. 'Yes, I suppose it would be much more staisfying to have me love my prison. Sorry—not even you can have everything.'

'That wasn't exactly what I meant.' He smiled without amusement and swung her neatly around an old friend who was revealing just how much of the excellent champagne he had drunk by the wildness of his dancing.

Once that obstacle had been negotiated he continued, 'Not that this is the time to discuss it.'

'There's nothing to discuss.'

'You are right, of course,' he agreed with suave and infuriating courtesy. 'In the words of a cliché so time-honoured one needn't be ashamed of using it, the bed has been made and we both have to lie in it. I plan to get as much enjoyment as I can from a basically unsound situation.'

'You sound like a lawyer.'

It was open and disdainful provocation and retribution was instant and brutal. He bent his head to kiss her and did not break it until her lips clung, unconsciously seeking to prolong the caress.

Someone whistled and there were cheers and jests, to all of which Eliot replied with that worldly self-confidence she found so enviable and so irritating.

'I dislike you intensely,' she said, smiling fiercely up into the dark, autocratic face.

'I know; a pity, as I rather like you. Still, that's nothing because what holds us together is something much less controllable than mere liking or disliking.'

'Lust.' She said the word delicately, investing it with a searing scorn which lingered between them.

'Exactly. Perhaps, after hunger, the most powerful appetite in the world. Just think, Tiffany, if we'd never met you would probably have married a nice boy who would have taken you three times a week with no frills and refinements, and you'd have dutifully accepted that and asked yourself, in between changing children's nappies and wondering where the next cent was coming from, just what it was that people made such a fuss of. And you would probably have comforted yourself with the thought that women were less highly sexed than men.'

'And you,' she said, pretending to smile and gazing up into the blazing heat of his eyes, 'would have married a nice, well-bred girl who was no threat to your peace of mind and given her two children and been fully in control of your life and therefore happy.'

She had hit a sensitive nerve; his expression did not change. To Ella, who was watching them openly, he would appear to be smiling affectionately down, but just for an instant the well-cut lips had tightened and something had flared briefly into life in his eyes.

'As you say,' he agreed, pulling her closer so that she rested against him. 'Do you think you would be happier with the humdrum life you might have chosen? I can give you much more than mere happiness, Tiffany.'

The dark shadings of his beautiful voice seduced her ears. It was difficult to struggle against it but she did.

'Chosen is the word,' she said, trying to make words as objective as possible. 'No one can expect happiness, or choose happiness. It's a by-product. But we should have the right to make our own decisions.' In spite of her care a note of passion crept into her words. 'It is not fair—you have no right to take the choice away from me.'

'Do you think I had any alternative?'

The bitter words etched themselves on to Tiffany's brain, seared into her soul. But she rallied. 'There is always a choice,' she said stubbornly.

Suddenly he laughed, flinging his head back as though she had amused him immensely. Only Tiffany could hear the sardonic appreciation in his laughter, only she heard the words that followed.

'And that, my darling, my dearest, my heart, is where you're wrong. That is what passion does, plays its joke on all of us so that there are no choices. Only it's a bitter joke, a practical joke that leaves one bankrupt of will. You say you despise me, Tiffany; you can't despise me any more than I do.

Her heart clenched in agony. He was suffering and his pain made him lash out. If only he could learn to love her! But it was useless to cry for the moon, just as it was useless to hope for anything other than bitter unhappiness in this life he was forcing on to her, because he saw his desire for her as a weakness, a flaw in the fabric of his personality, and he hated her for causing it.

A sigh wrenched its way through her. The strong arms about her tightened. In a strangely gentle voice he said, 'Relax, Tiffany. You know by now that fighting this useless battle will only exhaust you. We have so much—we could have so much if you would only give in. Another cliché I find rather comforting is that everything looks better in the morning.'

'I wish . . .' she said, but she didn't know what she wished, for his love was unattainable. Another forlorn sigh escaped her and he lifted her chin and said with a hint of imperious toughness, 'Now don't go looking like the lost princess, or people will think I beat you.'

'Do you care what people think?'

'Not in the least,' he said calmly. 'Or I wouldn't be marrying the woman most people are convinced was my uncle's light of love, would I? But it isn't done for lawyers to oppress the helpless, you know. It gives people the wrong impression.'

He was teasing her and she smiled in response, suddenly liking him very much. How many different ways there were to relate to him, a new emotion for each aspect of his character, she thought, as the music flowed sweetly around them and the rest of the party left them in their own world. Love, and desire, and liking; respect for a man who had been kind to his uncle and to the elderly woman who had sprained her ankle that night in the city. And there was hate and resentment, despair and cold anger. As well as this tenderness she felt. From the first she had appreciated the dilemma of a strong man who was forced by an overwhelming emotion to behave in a way which upset his understanding of his own character. It made his cruelty comprehensible, although not forgivable. But couldn't he see what he was condemning them both to? A life based on just one driving hunger must eventually collapse into its own emptiness.

Or is that what he expected? Sudden cold swept over her skin, chilling her. Did he hope that eventually the passion he saw as degrading would cloy so that he would regain his self-respect? Cold panic made her heart beat heavily in her ears, overriding the physical stimulus she always felt in his presence. I must get away, she thought wildly, at last seeing the pit of destruction he had set before her feet. Horrifying as it would be to be treated as a sexual toy it would be infinitely worse if the only bonds between them eventually snapped and he could look at her with indifference. I'd rather die, she thought with icy desperation. Oh God, I'd rather kill him and then myself than have to watch while he wearies of me and I look into his eyes and see only boredom and disgust.

No! I am being hysterical, she told herself firmly. Not Eliot, not the man she had come to love, so reluctantly, so sweetly. Eyes wide, she looked up into his face, wincing at the strength, the harsh arrogance of bone structure, the bleak, implacable blue of his eyes. He said nothing but smiled cruelly, sensing her desperation and enjoying it.

Yes, he would do that. He saw her as the witch Circe, who had turned men into pigs for their gross appetites.

She knew then what she had to do.

The party finished around three. Mrs Buchanan was openly yawning as she turned away from the door. 'Well, that was fun,' she said simply. 'You look tired, Tiffany. We should have organised you into staying the night.'

'It's not far.' Eliot kissed his mother's cheek, smiling at her with affection. 'Thank you.'

'For what? I love parties, you know that, and I specially loved this one. I've waited so long to see you in love!' Mrs Buchanan's shrewd glance lingered just too long on Tiffany's pale cheeks and downcast lashes. 'I'll ring you tomorrow, my dear, and we'll make final plans. When do you go south?'

'Next Wednesday,' Eliot replied for her, his voice cool and incisive. 'Come on, darling, you're just about out on your feet.'

His arm was strong and reassuring. Tiffany managed a smile and a thank you for his mother before she was led inexorably out to the car.

The city was still, no other car on the roads. Some time during the evening it had rained and the tarmac was slicked with water, hissing slightly under the wheels. The street lights glared emptily down at black, smooth pavements. Tiffany stared through the windscreen, screwing her courage to the sticking point.

But although he checked the house out as usual he bade her good night without anything more than a kiss, about as passionate as the one he had given his mother, on her forehead. Wearily, so exhausted that she wasn't even capable of relief that she had put off her decision, Tiffany climbed the stairs. Her feet hurt, her throat hurt and just under her breastbone there was a hard heavy lump which made it impossible for her to swallow.

But she slept as if she had been drugged. Not until after it was daylight did she begin to toss and whimper beneath her breath.

CHAPTER NINE

WHEN she woke it was with a blinding headache and a sense of coming doom so strong that even after she had walked Jess she was afflicted by it. The headache had eased but she felt cold and shivery, almost as if she was getting influenza.

When Eliot arrived she was huddled into the armchair drinking peppermint tea and talking to Jess, who was lying across her feet, eyeing her with faint alarm.

'You look like death,' he observed, holding her at arms length.

The small muscles in her throat moved spasmodically as she swallowed. When she at last managed to speak her voice sounded harsh yet faint.

'I'm—Eliot, I'm not going to marry you,' she said.

He went very still then the black brows drew together. 'We've been through all that,' he said calmly. 'You silly wench, have you been up all night steeling yourself?'

'I'm not going to marry you,' she repeated steadily, swaying slightly.

Instantly his hand came out to support her. At his touch she flinched. His fingers tightened unbearably, then relaxed and he said smoothly. 'Yes you are, my dear. You're tired and overwrought——'

'Stop treating me as though I were a hysterical teenager,' she snapped, gaining strength from her anger.

'You're acting rather like one.' The deep deliberate voice was tinged by mockery but his face was blank, although he was holding hard on a powerful emotion.

'No, I'm behaving with some common sense at last,' she told him evenly. 'If you won't accept that a marriage between us would be a disaster, then I must be

166

sensible. I'm not going to walk into a battlefield and wait to die.'

He smiled, very sure of himself, very condescending. 'What a dramatic little mind you have, my lovely. I promise you that I have no intention of killing you.'

'Marriage with you would be a slow death,' she stated sturdily, backing away from him as he came towards her.

'You're talking nonsense, and you know it.' His eyes were on her mouth and as she turned her head away she saw the sudden flames irradiate the blue depths.

'No!' she gasped, but he laughed and took her by the shoulders and kissed her without mercy and without tenderness, forcing her to accept him.

Only when she was heavy-eyed and trembling, her breathing thick in her panting chest, did he lift his head. And then it was to run his hand down to her hips and press them against him so that her body jerked in arousal and desire.

'There,' he said thickly, triumph and satisfaction equally blended in his voice. 'Now tell me that you don't want me.'

'I didn't say that I didn't want you.' She lifted her lashes and stared at him, calling on her reserves of courage and strength to carry her through the next hour. 'I want you—unbearably. You know that. But I'm not going to marry you.'

He held her gaze for long moments, his own giving nothing away. Then he let her go and demanded, 'Tell me why.'

'I've told you why. Sex is all that we've got.' And more in the belief that she would be convinced at the rightness of her actions than in the hope that he might feel more than lust for her she continued, 'It fades, I don't need to tell you that. You've had enough affairs to know that anything palls after a while. What happens to us when you've had enough of me? You say you won't divorce me but I'm not going to live with you knowing that you hate me and don't want me. Do you think I'm a masochist?'

'I think you're a stupid woman,' he said blightingly, his anger rising to match hers. 'Or perhaps a stupid little girl would be a better term to describe you. Have you thought what you'll be doing to your mother if you don't marry me?'

'Why won't you answer me?' she whispered.

The shutters came down, all signs of emotion wiped clear from the harsh, strong features. From beneath his lashes he watched her consideringly. She knew then that her suppositions of the night before had been correct. He could inflict so much damage to her personality that she would never be whole again.

'I'm not going to marry you,' she said heavily. She pulled the beautiful ring he had chosen from her finger and held it out to him, her hand trembling.

'Working on the principle that "what I say three times I say true",' he said, making no move to take it.

'I mean it.'

He nodded. 'Yes, I can see that you do.' The hard blue of his gaze flicked across to the flight of stairs then back to her pale, set face. 'I could make you change your mind.'

'No,' she said, shaking her head. Her hair felt damp, she pushed her free hand through the thick curls and felt the sweat there. 'No, you could make love to me until I'm witless with wanting you, but I won't change my mind.'

At last he took the ring, head bent as he turned the lovely thing in his fingers so that the dull light through the windows was caught and enhanced into a glittering mass of light and colour.

'Very well then, there's nothing more to be said.'

Tiffany's hands flew to her heart. She had expected— oh, she had expected to be brow-beaten, threatened, menaced. This calm acceptance bewildered her. Unspeaking she watched as he walked across the room to the door, the lithe body gracefully erect, moving with the spare smoothness he had made his. Jess frisked at his feet, but he avoided her without seeming to.

As he reached the door he said calmly, 'You needn't worry about your mother's secret. I have no intention of telling her husband.'

Her ears were filled by the drumming of her heart. She could feel it beneath her hand, beating so heavily that it seemed it must break through its prison of flesh and bone; it prevented her from hearing what he said to Jess but she heard him call, and call again, and she was already running when she heard the squeal of brakes and a short, interrupted yelp.

'Stay there,' Eliot called over his shoulder but she was just behind him when he got to the car and its protesting, shaken driver.

'Thank God I was hardly moving,' she said, stooping to the little bundle of fur which was Jess. 'It can't be dead, surely?'

Eliot's strong, sure hands touched the short limbs and still body. 'No,' he said after a moment, his eyes intent. 'She's alive. A broken rib or two, perhaps, that's all.'

He stood up, and Tiffany only then realised that tears were running down her face. 'Darling,' he said gently. 'Go and ring this number, will you. It's our vet. I'll get her into the car.'

Two hours later they were back, Jess bruised but calm, still dopey after the sedative she had been given. As she had to be kept quiet and still for a time the vet had provided them with a cage which Eliot put down in a patch of sunlight by the sliding door.

'It's stupid to get so fond of them,' Tiffany said shakily.

'Why? She's an affectionate little thing, loving and full of fun. You'd have to be very hard of heart to feel nothing for her. And you're not hard-hearted, are you, Tiffany?'

'When I heard the car—I thought, *that's it*! I've got nothing now, it's all gone.' It was a damning little betrayal forced from her by shock.

But Eliot said easily, 'Oh, she's a survivor, this one.

Don't worry about her. Sit down, I'll make you some coffee.'

It gave Tiffany time to compose herself. As he moved quietly around the small kitchen she watched, her heart in her eyes, while around her the room grew warm, sunlight expanding within it in a glowing explosion of colour. Tiffany drank the coffee he brought her, listening to his voice. He was manipulating her in the best way, easing her shock with his quiet, uncontroversial conversation.

'You have consummate skill in managing people,' she observed gratefully after the coffee had wrought its heartening effect.

His lazy smile gave his expression an unexpected softness. 'It's on the curriculum at law school. Tiffany, what made you decide to jilt me this morning?'

'I couldn't bear to live with you and see whatever it is that we have dwindle into indifference and hatred,' she said, tiredness and stress forcing an honesty she would almost certainly regret later.

'Why should it?'

'Isn't that what usually happens? You need to love, unselfishly and generously, to live happily ever after. And even then it doesn't always work out.'

He had been leaning against the glass door but at this he straightened up. 'So?' he asked softly. 'Don't you know yet, you silly little rabbit, that I'm in love with you? Quite—*unbearably*—in love with you? And have been, I think, almost from the first time I saw you.'

Tiffany stared at him, her eyes dilated with shock. 'I don't believe you,' she said numbly, because something had to be said.

He shrugged. 'I find it hard to believe myself. But it's true.'

She looked away from the dark glitter of his gaze, linking her hands tightly in her lap to stop the tremors which shook them. 'Not—not right from the first. You thought I was a tramp. You said so.'

He grimaced. 'If I remember correctly I said you were

a pretty little tramp. And if I didn't fall in love with you why didn't I just walk away from you? Because I couldn't. I wanted you rather more than I wanted to eat and sleep and breathe.'

'Why?' She lifted her eyes to meet his. He looked coolly amused, as though they were enjoying a flirtatious conversation. 'No, I mean it, Eliot. I'm not your usual sort of woman. Why should you love me?'

'Perhaps because you're not my usual sort.' He came to sit beside her, carefully avoiding any contact between them. 'You've met Ella. She's the usual sort. Beautiful, quite clever, hard enough so that our affair wouldn't put a scratch on her heart. Eminently desirable.'

Tiffany felt a surge of vicious jealousy which made her close her eyes.

'I do know why I love you,' he said, smiling slightly. 'But why you turn me on so hard that I damned near raped you—I don't know the reason for that. Chemistry? Hormones? All I know is that when I saw you that first time, sitting so primly beside Geoffrey with the sun tangled in your curls, I felt a jolt of recognition. As though you were mine. As though once we'd been all in all to each other and then been torn apart and finally, after aeons of searching, we'd found each other again.'

He was wooing her with all his charm of voice and manner, the seductive words enchaining her heart and imagination. Tiffany couldn't bear his nearness. His confession of love was so unexpected that she wasn't able to accept it yet. Jumping to her feet she said hoarsely, 'But that wasn't—you were an absolute swine to me.'

'Naturally. You were obviously involved with Geoffrey. I couldn't believe that it was sexual yet there seemed no other explanation, the bond between you was so strong. I was totally, savagely, racked with jealousy.' His voice was sombre with remembered pain. 'I hated being anywhere near you.'

'Yet you came to see Geoffrey.'

He looked up at her, his expression remote. 'Those evenings were when I fell in love with you. You were spirited and independent and intelligent. I wanted it all, your warmth and your kindness, everything that was you. You used to smile at Geoffrey—I would have knelt for a smile like that from you.'

'If I'd known . . .' she said half under her breath. 'I suppose I fell in love with you, then, too. I just didn't recognise it.'

'Then why,' he asked carefully, 'did you refuse to marry me?'

She gave him a twisted smile. 'Because your damned honour made you propose! I wanted—I *want* much more from you than you offered me then. I want you, not just the pleasure you can give me. I'm greedy. If I can't have you with no conditions, no barriers—well, that's why I said I'd be your mistress. At least that way I knew what to expect.'

There was a long silence. Eliot appeared to be considering her words, that clever quick brain turning them over, searching for every nuance of meaning.

When he looked up he was smiling without humour. 'Shall I tell you what I feel for you?'

'If you want to,' she said cautiously.

He gave an odd, clipped laugh, as though her answer had winded him, before leaning back into the sofa cushions, hands in his pockets, his long legs stretched out before him. It was exactly the way he had sat on the park bench the day he had, in effect, declared war on her. And, exactly as he had then, he looked dangerous.

Harshly he said, 'I can manipulate words with the best of them but when I try to imagine my life without you my tongue cleaves to the roof of my mouth. If you left me . . .' Incredibly, he stopped and swallowed hard. He was not looking at her; indeed, his eyes were fixed on the floor. 'The thought terrifies me. I daren't imagine it. It is impossible for me to conceive of any sort of existence without you.'

Tiffany moved uneasily. It was difficult for her to

believe that this was her cynical, sophisticated Eliot speaking with such sombre intensity that he compelled belief. Exultation gripped her, to be replaced immediately by fear. Only twice before he had been stripped of his self-sufficiency and each time he had turned on her, savaging her with his words.

He looked up into her face and made a muffled noise deep in his throat. 'My heart's dearest, how can I convince you?' he pleaded. 'I've behaved like a brute and a bully, terrorising you because I was bitterly, savagely jealous of what you shared with Geoffrey. Can't you believe that the strength of my feelings is some indication of the power you possess over them?'

'But as soon as you discovered who I was you knew that there was nothing to be jealous of,' she said quietly.

He sighed and hunched forward, putting out a hand to clasp hers and pull her beside him. His face remained resolutely turned away from her as if he dared not look at her, as if his nearness prevented the quick logical processes of his brain from functioning.

'All of your affection and smiles and concern were for Geoffrey. I wanted it for myself. Have you any idea what jealousy can do?'

'A little,' she admitted, thinking guiltily of the acid resentment she had conceived for Ella.

'I'm glad. At least that makes two of us to suffer it. For me it was the first time. I'd never thought enough of any woman to resent it if her attentions weren't exclusively mine.' His voice hardened into cold self-mockery as he turned to slide his arm across her shoulders, urging her sideways until she rested against him. He bent his head so that he spoke into her neck, his breath playing erotically across her skin. 'It was bitter servitude, an enslavement of my senses. I had to keep visiting Geoffrey because that was the only way I could see you but oh, God, I envied him so much that the affection of a lifetime was swamped by this—this degrading bondage. I despised myself but I hated you.

You weakened me, you appealed to my lowest urges—I think I nearly went mad for a while.'

Appalled, Tiffany drew a shuddering breath. The raw humiliation in his voice warned her that for all of his professed love for her he still saw his emotions as a weakness. Some day when he could bear to tell her she would discover why; for the moment she wanted only to comfort him.

Shyly, she enfolded his hand in her small, capable ones, gripping hard on the lean fingers. They flexed before returning her hold.

'I'm sorry,' she said. 'All things considered, you were—gentle with me. You were in such a dangerous mood that you must have felt like killing me.'

For a split second his grip tightened unbearably. 'Not exactly,' he said sombrely. 'It wasn't your death I wanted. But it was that combination of lust and anger which made me rape you.'

'Is that what you meant when you said that there was an excuse for any deed, however horrible? Remember, you made me admit that given the right circumstances I could kill?'

'In a way, I suppose so. Only——' his mouth branded her neck, moving with heated ardour over the soft skin, 'I fuelled my fantasies by imagining you completely at my mercy. I used to pretend that I would drive you insane with my lovemaking and then spurn you, leaving you panting and pleading at my feet. But all the time I knew that I would never have the strength to walk away. And that instead of rejecting you I'd give my life, my honour, my heart for you.'

Tiffany sat very still, her breath stopped in her body. Very slowly she turned her head, pulling it back so that she could focus on his face.

'No,' she whispered. 'Not like that—*no!* I don't—I'm not strong enough——'

'Do you think I *want* to feel like that?' He spoke more swiftly than she had ever known him to speak, each word clear and incisive while his eyes blazed into hers. 'There's nothing I can do about it. I've heard of *femmes fatales*, but I never believed in such a fatal attraction until I found it in you.'

'Oh, *God*,' she moaned and as the tears came to her eyes she pulled his head down and smothered him with kisses, whispering in between each one, 'I'm sorry, I'm sorry . . .' until he silenced the soft pleas for forgiveness with his mouth.

'Why should you be sorry?' He spoke quietly against her lips, holding her close across his lap. 'It isn't your fault.'

'I misjudged you so. I didn't know. I didn't realise . . .'

'I know. I knew then.' The hard mouth curved into a smile. 'If you had realised you'd have been a lot more frightened of me than you were.'

She nodded. 'You seemed so sophisticated, too worldly to suffer from the kind of torrid emotions that were tearing me to bits. When you did take me I was——' She stopped, her skin heating as she remembered. 'I was—angry, but—enraptured,' she admitted slowly. 'But you were furious. I thought it was because I'd made you lose your self-control.'

His narrowed gaze glittered as it rested on the soft sensual curve of her lips. 'You were right. You were so sweetly abandoned, so innocently wanton, and I couldn't get enough of you.'

His lashes came down and hid his eyes. After a moment he looked at her. Tonelessly he said, 'I suppose I was about fifteen when I realised that my father was unfaithful to my mother. I found her weeping one day; she made some excuse but I knew she was lying. A few days later I overheard a couple of my father's friends talking. It appeared that he couldn't resist a pretty face. Or some pretty faces. When I was older I discovered that there hadn't been many, but every so often he would lapse. He made my mother bitterly unhappy.'

'I see,' she said quietly And she did see, at last.

'Being young and brash I tackled him about them,'

he went on with bitter scorn. 'He said they meant nothing. He adopted a detestably man-to-man attitude towards me. To be honest I really believe that to him they didn't mean anything. He loved my mother as much as he was able. He believed that men were polygamous by nature.'

In spite of herself Tiffany couldn't prevent a small sound of contempt from escaping her lips. 'And do you?' she asked fiercely.

'No.' He laughed down into her face, brushing her lips with his. 'No,' he whispered into her mouth, 'I want only one woman. Since I met you there has been no one else.'

She stared up at him, wondering if he had tried, remembering Ella's beauty and her own anguish after that night. She had imagined them making love and she had been riven with a savage jealousy. She did not care now. Trust bloomed in her expression, made him draw a sharp hurting breath.

'Good,' she said fiercely, and turned her head into his shoulder. 'Tell me all about your horrid father.'

'I think you can guess. I blamed him for not having the self-control to restrain himself. He chose women younger than him, women who knew their way about. In his way he was quite honourable. He stressed that no gentleman ever seduced an innocent. But you can see why I felt such revulsion when I saw you with Geoffrey.'

'Yes,' she sighed, listening to the heavy thud of his heart.

'Then I took you,' he said thinly. 'I hadn't meant to. I thought that although you made my guts twist with desire I'd have the strength to leave you alone. So I had to face the fact that I was no better than my father. Will-power, restraint, self-control—the foundations I'd built my life on were flawed, worth nothing. Making love to you was the most exciting thing that had ever happened to me and afterwards I lay beside you and realised that you had been a virgin and I'd treated you like a whore.'

'No,' she exclaimed. 'No, Eliot—it wasn't like that.'

He smiled mirthlessly at the horror on her face. 'Yes,' he said. 'I'd given you no choice, forced you. And because I was sick with self-contempt I lashed out at you. Woman, the eternal enemy, the weakener; Lilith who sucked men dry of all honour.'

In her box Jess rolled from her back to her side, paws twitching, her eyelids jerking as she chased a dream rabbit through pastures never seen on this earth. Beyond her the plants in the garden moved gently in the wind, the silvery, almond-green new growth in the deciduous trees a gentle background to clumps of irises and freesias. A crimson japonica glowed with artistic informality against the wall; separated from it by a small evergreen bush with white star-shaped flowers was a poinsettia, vivid, brilliant through the gloom. Low cloud scudded by at hill-top level. The sun had gone in and it was cold, prematurely dark; soon the lights would go on. But next month it would be spring.

'Why did you tell me I had to marry you?' Tiffany asked.

'I told myself that it was my duty, because I wouldn't, couldn't admit that I didn't want to face life without you.' His hand on her back clenched. 'It didn't occur to me that you'd refuse.'

'Another black mark.' She reached up a hand to run it caressingly over his jaw. Beneath her fingers the fine skin tightened. 'I couldn't accept. I thought—I was sure—that you couldn't love me. I was terrified. I thought that I would go mad trapped in the kind of marriage you offered me. You seemed to hate me yet want me. I was petrified,' she repeated.

'Yes.' He kissed the palm of her hand, brought it up to hold it against his mouth in a caress as tender as it was sensual.

Tiffany met the brilliant blue eyes without flinching. One part of her longed for this to be over so that they could lose themselves in the silent world of passion they had made their own, but she knew that passion by itself was worthless. This was what was important, this communication, this meeting of minds and hearts. It was difficult for her to tell him of her cowardice, the repressions and fears which had prevented her from accepting her emotions honestly and ardently; she could tell that it was hard for him, too, to face the less pleasant aspects of his character. Yet because he loved her he was not only doing that but sharing them with her.

Shyly, her emotions transparent, she smiled into his eyes, saw an answering tenderness which blocked her throat.

'Oh, God, I love you,' he said raggedly. 'I never thought—I didn't know that I could love like this. Before it's just been plain desire and liking. I've always been the one who called the tune. I didn't believe in the love the poets rave about.' He laughed beneath his breath and kissed her, then set her back on to the sofa and got up to walk restlessly across the room.

Tiffany's eyes followed him. It was too soon to gaze at him openly. She was used to snatching brief glances to satisfy her greedy heart. Now from beneath her lashes she watched the play of muscles as he walked, the set of the wide shoulders above the narrow waist and hips, the lean, strongly-muscled thighs and arms, and she felt a wave of desire so strong that it almost swamped her. Unconsciously her tongue slid along her lips; her lashes flickered as she dragged her eyes back to the hands in her lap.

How did he do it? It was not so much his body, although that was physically perfect, or the formidable attraction of his features. Even the charm he used like a weapon didn't explain it. It was, she thought, the explicit, open promise every woman sensed in him. Without words, he promised physical pleasure to any woman who shared his bed. His masculinity called to femininity at the most basic, the most primitive level.

And femininity responded. She had seen how Ella Sheridan reacted to him. Last night had proved that it was not an isolated reaction. Every woman in the room had been aware of him, tuned to his presence.

Yet he had chosen her, not because he wanted to but because he could not help himself. So intensely male himself he had found his perfect complement in her. A glow of love and trust sparked in her eyes, banished the weariness from her face.

He looked at her. 'Yes,' he said almost calmly. 'I couldn't believe that my happiness depended on a girl I'd disdained as not particularly pretty, not even very clever. You had no sophisticated repartee, you didn't even know the little tricks to arouse a man's interest and yet at night I dreamt of you. I'd wake hurting with need and desire. You obsessed me; I found myself going over and over our lovemaking, planning ways to make it better for you next time. If there ever was a next time.'

He swung to look at her, his expression as haughty and disdainful as it had been on that first meeting, his eyes blazing with accusation. 'You came between me and my work, you haunted me, you reduced me in my own eyes. I kept away but the thought of you ate at my self-control like acid. And I still wouldn't admit that I loved you. The only way I could keep some sort of pride was to tell myself that you'd marry me and when that happened I'd sate myself with you, take you until you were no more to me than any other woman I'd had.'

So she had been right last night. It didn't matter now.

'Beast,' she said softly, without censure.

His mouth twisted into a smile without humour. 'Oh, yes. Underneath it all, of course, I was running scared. That was why I persuaded you into going out with me. I deliberately flirted with you and flattered you, took you to places to see how you'd behave. I was glad to see that you possessed a quiet dignity which carried you through any situation. You could, I decided in my arrogance, be shaped into a suitable wife. And you obviously were not indifferent to me. You tried to hide it but your response to me was sweet and spontaneous and very, very exciting.'

He smiled sardonically at the stunned face she showed him. 'And then,' he said softly, 'you turned down my proposal again and said, oh, so haughtily, that you'd take me as a lover. You kicked me in the heart and smiled as you did it. And it didn't make it any less painful that I deserved it.'

Tiffany got up and walked across to the kitchen. 'I'll make some more coffee,' she said, trying hard to grapple with this picture he had presented to her of himself.

In the automatic movements she found some comfort. When the coffee was ready she took him a cup and said gravely, 'Why weren't you pleased, Eliot? As my lover you could—sate yourself without losing pride or your freedom.'

He looked down into the coffee before moving to set it down on the chest. Even like this, stiff with tension, his body moved with lithe grace. Colour flooded Tiffany's skin as she remembered the weight of him pressing her into the bed, the fierce energy which overwhelmed them both as they made love, the painful, ecstatic tide of sensation those strong hands and that cruel mouth could wring from her body. Deep inside her, like an ache, she felt passion kindle and burn, weakening her limbs, shadowing her slumberous eyes.

He stood half-turned away from her, the clean, harsh lines of his profile hawk-like against the rain outside. When he spoke his voice was light, almost derisive.

'It was made abundantly clear to me that I wasn't going to be satisfied with the usual liaison. Sex and entertainment was not enough. As my mistress you would have kept your freedom, too, able to walk out on me whenever you wanted. I was appalled and scared to realise that what I wanted was you shackled so fast to me that you couldn't escape. I wanted you as enslaved as I was.' The deep, beautiful voice paused, then continued deliberately, 'As I am.'

Her heart leapt in her breast. She swallowed, her mouth and throat dry with strain. He stood with his proud head bent, not looking at her.

Almost as if he was afraid.

And then he lifted his head and turned it so that she could see the naked appeal in his expression and she said shakily, 'How silly we've been, both of us. Don't you know that I would kill myself if you asked me to? I thought that it was hatred and desire which bound us together but I should have known that only love could be so powerful.'

'Tiffany.' He took a step towards her, his hand outstretched. 'Tiffany,' he said again, his voice lingering huskily over the syllables. 'My dear delight. My heart.'

They met, and kissed, and kissed again, like lovers denied each other's presence for too long. Tiffany did as she had longed to, ran her fingers through his hair, pressing herself against him with open sensuality while her heart slammed with thick, heavy strokes in her breast and her body twisted against him, innocently provocative, inviting the ultimate embrace.

'No,' he whispered, lifting his head at last. 'Stop it, darling.'

She lifted her lashes, her expression surprised. 'Why?'

'Because next time it's going to be perfect for us, and that means after we're married.' He lifted her and carried her across to the sofa, smiling down at her with a fierce possessiveness which thrilled her.

'I've discovered,' he said, coming down beside her, 'that I can't separate my brain and my body. At least, not without tearing myself apart. When I took you that first time I blindly allowed my passions free reign, and bitterly regretted it. The second time I deliberately set out to seduce you into submission. I tried to use the pleasure I could give you as a lever to force you to marry me. I used every trick I knew, called on every ounce of expertise to reduce you to surrender.'

'I noticed,' she said quietly, pulling him down beside her. 'You were—I was dazzled, I thought that I'd never

know such rapture, such ecstasy again. It was perfect—
but impersonal. I preferred the first time.'

He looked startled. 'But I hurt you—forced you into
making love.'

Tiffany smiled and nuzzled her face into his shoulder.
His arm tightened; she felt his chest move as he took a
deep breath.

'Yes, but you wanted me,' she told him. 'So much
that you lost control. The second time you knew exactly
what you were doing all of the time. It was like—oh,
like a pianist with a fabulous technique and no passion,
no emotion.'

'There was passion and emotion enough,' he said
grimly. 'I didn't dare let go because I was afraid of
hurting you again.'

She said nothing but lifted her hand and traced the
outline of his lips with her finger.

After a moment he said harshly. 'And because I
wanted to prove to myself that I wasn't weak and
totally lacking in control where you were concerned.'

'And because you were angry and you needed to
punish me.'

He nodded, slanting her a quick, mocking glance.
'Oh, yes, that too. I suppose I was clinging rather
desperately to my superiority. It wasn't until I faced the
truth that I realised that my pride had to go.'

'And the truth was?'

'Just that I love you.' He turned and pushed her
down into the cushions, stretching himself beside her.
The sofa was not wide enough to take them both but
Tiffany welcomed the beloved weight of his body as he
lowered himself half on to her. His strong clever hands
shaped her face, touched her throat and shoulders and
breasts. He looked remote, his face hard and self-
sufficient until he lifted his lashes and she saw the need
which darkened his eyes.

'Just love,' he said again quietly. 'When I accepted
that, nothing else mattered except that you love me
too.'

It was strange to hear him almost asking for reassurance. She had never thought to hear him like this; in an obscure way it hurt to hear her arrogant lover being humble.

'Oh, I do,' she said softly, pulling his head down on to her breast so that she could stroke the crisp hair. 'This side of idolatry. But you knew that, didn't you?'

'I hoped. God knows why you should——'

She laughed wryly. 'Because I'm a masochist, of course. The fact that you are strong and kind and fierce, handsome and clever, and you like dogs and children and old people and that I fancy you so much that I only have to look at you and I want to go to bed with you, has nothing to do with loving you.'

'This side of idolatry?' He sounded shaken. 'That's beyond idolatry, my lovely girl. I hope I can make you happy all the years we have together.'

'Oh, I think you'll manage,' she told him softly. 'I think you'll manage very well. Just be around. That's all it will take.'

They kissed, long and satisfactorily and then she laid a finger on his lips and asked, 'Eliot, why did my—why did Geoffrey's children decide not to contest the will?'

'Because I persuaded them not to.'

She nodded, not very surprised. 'How—and why?'

'How? I pointed out that contesting the will would delay probate and as they were both in rather desperate need of money that was a strong inducement to be reasonable. As for the why of it . . .' He shrugged, smiling. 'I wanted you cared for. I hated to think of you struggling along on a tiny wage, taking in extra sewing. You see, I didn't realise that you were an entrepreneur, quite capable of making a very nice living for yourself without my help. Later, when I realised who you were I was glad. I told Diane and Colin, incidentally.'

Her mouth formed an 'o' of surprise and he kissed it and then said, 'I also told them that if anyone found out from them who you were I'd see that you got the third of the estate you were entitled to as Geoffrey's daughter. Greed being their besetting sin, they'll keep quiet.'

She nodded. 'It's strange, they are my half-brother and sister yet I have nothing in common with them. I don't even like them very much.'

'You won't be seeing much of them, and when you do, they'll behave.'

He meant it, too. For a moment he was the Eliot Buchanan she had first met, hard, ruthless, his expression grim. Then it softened as he smiled into her eyes. 'Don't worry about them,' he said, kissing the soft spot below her ear. 'You made Geoffrey very happy before he died. Just remember that.'

CHAPTER TEN

IT should have been a small wedding; that was the plan. But in a country district there is no such thing as a small wedding. In the end they were married with all Tiffany's friends and neighbours there, and a surprising number of Eliot's relations and friends, too, startling and amusing the locals with their elegance and worldliness.

'I'm sure that the whole affair only confirmed your friends' opinions that you've gone mad,' Tiffany teased that night, turning to him in the sitting room of the chalet he had borrowed from friends.

He laughed and came to her and slipped his arms around her. 'It wasn't that I saw in their faces. Envy, that was what was there. Not a man in the congregation did anything but wish he was in my shoes.'

'Even Alex Thomassin?'

'Ah, but he's besotted with his Christabel.'

She nodded. 'It was nice to see them here.'

'I barely noticed them.' He kissed the spot where her neck joined her shoulder, his hands tracing with sure lightness the line of breast and waist and hip.

Tiffany's breath hurt in her chest. She was starved for him. But she knew from his touch that he would not rush her into the enormous double bed upstairs; he would savour these minutes in a long, slow build-up of tension until he could no longer control his passion.

The chalet looked out over lovely Queenstown and the snow-covered Remarkable Mountains across the narrow deep waters of Lake Wakitipu. Not far away was the Coronet Peak ski-field; some time in the two weeks they were to spend here they might ski there. Perhaps.

A slow, secret smile touched Tiffany's lips. Perhaps. She leaned her head back on to his shoulder.

'How strong you are,' she murmured. 'Strong and sure and warm. Your heart is the most comforting sound I've ever heard. When I woke up after that night you cared for me so gently, when I was sick, I was cuddled into your side and I listened to your heart. I wondered how I could feel so—so safe when I despised you and feared you. If I'd had a little more experience I suppose I'd have realised much sooner that I was blindly, besottedly, in love with you.'

'Oh, I don't know.' He sounded amused and rueful at the same time. 'I was just as obtuse and heaven knows, I'd had enough experience.'

'But not of love,' she pointed out, surprised to find that she felt no goad of jealousy.

'No,' he muttered into her hair. 'Not of love. Did you know that your stepfather warned me last night to take care of you?'

'No!' She tilted her head but he held it still.

'Yes. He said that he'd never seen you so radiant and that he didn't want to see it diminish. I think my reputation as a womaniser must have preceded me.'

'Oh.' She knew how he would have hated that. 'What did you say?'

He laughed softly. 'Oh, I think I managed to convince him that whatever my life was like before I met you, from now on all that I want to do is make you happy.'

Tiffany put up a hand to his face, curved it lovingly around the high plane of his cheek, the autocratic jaw. 'It's an awesome responsibility, isn't it?' she said solemnly.

'It is, indeed. What were you and your mother discussing so earnestly before we left?'

Tiffany was silent for a moment then she said slowly, 'She was telling me that before I came home she told my stepfather about Geoffrey and me.'

'And?'

'He'd known all the time, Eliot. He'd waited all these years for her to tell him.' Tiffany's eyes filled with tears and her voice shook. 'I've often thought that he was—

too rigid, too hard and narrow, but I was so wrong. He must love her an awful lot to wait so patiently for her to confide in him.'

'Of course he does.' Eliot, too, was moved. His hands on her shoulders turned her into his arms. With his mouth just a breath away from hers he said gently, 'Your step-father recognised himself in me. He knew that I was like him, a man who would only love once, and then totally and completely, without reservations or conditions.'

Tiffany frowned even as she thrilled to the cool words delivered in his most toneless voice. 'As I love you,' she said. 'But if he knew that, darling, why did he warn you?'

His mouth touched the corner of hers. She could feel it move as he spoke, his voice held steady by his immense restraint. 'Because we tend to dominate. Because we find it hard to share. Because we resent even the sort of smiles I saw you bestow on your old boyfriends today.'

Tiffany started and jerked her head back. His voice had been flat but beneath his lashes his narrowed eyes glittered.

'Do you think I didn't know who they were?' he asked, and for a moment there was cold irony in his gaze before it softened. 'I could become insanely jealous of anything you like, anyone you spend time with,' he said quietly. 'That was what George warned me about. I want to possess you, your every thought and emotion and sensation like a Turkish pasha with his favourite concubine whose very existence depends on pleasing only him. You said once that I smothered you—I could, very easily.'

Tiffany stared at him, aware only now of the immense responsibility that his love laid on her. For a moment she felt crushed by it, then she looked deeper into the vivid blue of his eyes and saw there the question he was asking and she knew that she was strong enough.

'No you couldn't,' she said softly, her mouth tender. 'All you have to do is remember that I fell in love with you when you were behaving like that Turkish pasha, being as difficult and dominating as you could possibly be. I love you beyond the sex thing; I love you because you are strong and kind and considerate and I knew when I saw you first that you were a man I could lose my heart to. Why do you think I was so prickly and wary?'

He smiled. 'I think that was the sex thing you're so scathing about,' he said and very gently and sensuously bit her earlobe.

Tiffany's heart raced. Her hand moved down his face to the sinewed length of his throat. Beneath her soft touch she felt his pulse-rate pick up speed.

'No,' she said urgently. 'No. It was more than that. Because you cared enough for Geoffrey to go out of your way to take him to his appointment.' His mouth moved slowly, oh, so slowly, from her tingling ear to her eyes.

'I can't think,' she said desperately, wanting nothing more than to succumb to the erotic sensations which flooded her body. But although he was deliberately doing this to her she knew that she had to convince him.

'Don't talk,' he whispered. 'The time for talking is past. Show me.'

Before he had been the aggressor, the one with the experience to initiate their love play. But now it was she who touched him, carefully freeing the buttons on his beautiful shirt to run her hands over the width of his chest and shoulders, her expression absorbed as she committed the feel of him to memory. She swayed closer and began to kiss the smooth skin, her fingers parting the fine hairs which emphasised the width and strength of his chest.

Beneath her lips the wall of his chest rose and fell sharply.

'Let's go up,' he said thickly and picked her up.

The house was centrally heated, so the sudden shiver she gave was not due to any fall of temperature. When he set her on her feet she held his hand against her breast where her heart thundered.

'I love you,' she said, and said it again when they lay together in the big bed, their bodies twisting, his breathing heavy and harsh as his mouth roamed her breasts and the narrow span of her waist.

She said it again in that first moment of exquisite sensation as his body reinforced his mastery of hers in thrusting power, sobbed the words later, barely knowing that they meant as her hands clenched on the tense muscles of his back. It was then in anguish that he lost control, mind and body bent only on one thing, the sating of himself in the warmth that was her.

And when, exhausted, his breathing beginning to normalise, he lay pressing her into the big bed she said it again, pushing back the sweat-dampened hair from his forehead, her whole being lapped in relaxed, diffused warmth.

'Convinced now?' she murmured into his shoulder.

He moved, turning on to his side so that he could pull her against him. 'Oh yes,' he muttered. 'When you give, you give everything, don't you? Heart, soul and body. I've never known such—such loving generosity. You make me feel like the king of the world.'

She chuckled, pressing her face into his shoulder, reacting with delight as he tensed against her touch. 'I thought that making love was supposed to exhaust you,' she teased.

'Whatever gave you that idea?'

He was laughing but beneath it was tenderness and the hot tension of desire and something else, a deep current of love. Tiffany sighed her relief and kissed him, looping her arm under his so that it stretched across his back. He began to speak, the syllables lazy and quiet in the quiet room, wooing her only with his voice and the soft, sensuous brush of his fingers from her ribs to her hip. She was enchanted by his words, the deep, resonant voice making magic for her in this enchanted night. But as her body responded to his caresses, she felt a profound gratitude. There was no holding back now; he was revealing his innermost self to her, confident at last that she would not reject him or misuse her power, just as she knew that he would never do so to her. They had come home, and home was each other.

ROMANCE

Variety is the spice of romance

Each month, Mills & Boon publish new romances. New stories about people falling in love. A world of variety in romance — from the best writers in the romantic world. Choose from these titles in March.

RECKLESS Amanda Carpenter
MAN IN THE PARK Emma Darcy
AN UNBREAKABLE BOND Robyn Donald
ONE IN A MILLION Sandra Field
DIPLOMATIC AFFAIR Claire Harrison
POWER POINT Rowan Kirby
DARK BETRAYAL Patricia Lake
NO LONGER A DREAM Carole Mortimer
A SCARLET WOMAN Margaret Pargeter
A LASTING KIND OF LOVE Catherine Spencer
*__BLUEBELLS ON THE HILL__ Barbara McMahon
*__RETURN TO FARAWAY__ Valerie Parv

On sale where you buy paperbacks. If you require further information or have any difficulty obtaining them, write to: Mills & Boon Reader Service, PO Box 236, Thornton Road, Croydon, Surrey CR9 3RU, England.

*These two titles are available *only* from Mills & Boon Reader Service.

Mills & Boon the rose of romance

ROMANCE

Next month's romances from Mills & Boon

Each month, you can choose from a world of variety in romance with Mills & Boon. These are the new titles to look out for next month.

SOME SAY LOVE Lindsay Armstrong
CAPTIVES OF THE PAST Robyn Donald
CAPABLE OF FEELING Penny Jordan
THE PLUMED SERPENT Annabel Murray
A GIRL NAMED ROSE Betty Neels
BEYOND REACH Margaret Pargeter
A RISKY BUSINESS Sandra K. Rhoades
MISLEADING ENCOUNTER Jessica Steele
GAME OF HAZARD Kate Walker
LIKE ENEMIES Sophie Weston
*****THE RIGHT TIME** Maura McGiveny
*****THE TIGER'S CAGE** Margaret Way

Buy them from your usual paperback stockist, or write to: Mills & Boon Reader Service, P.O. Box 236, Thornton Rd, Croydon, Surrey CR9 3RU, England. Readers in South Africa write to: Mills & Boon Reader Service of Southern Africa, Private Bag X3010, Randburg, 2125.

*These two titles are available *only* from Mills & Boon Reader Service.

Mills & Boon
the rose of romance

NEW LONGER HISTORICAL ROMANC

You'll be carried away by The Passionate Pirate.

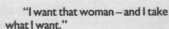

"I want that woman – and I take what I want."

And so the beautiful, headstrong Angelina Blackthorne is abducted by th very man who she held responsible for her father's ruin.

Alone and vulnerable, she falls victim to his ruthless desires.

Yet try as she might, she can't hate him as she feels she should … in the way he so rightly deserves.

'The Passionate Pirate': available from 11th April 1986.

Price £1.50.

MASQUERAD